A NEW BEGINNING

When Kirsty Johnston visits Fells Inn it's no longer the happy place of her childhood memories, but run-down and up for sale. The only other guest is the mysterious Bob, who keeps to himself. Despite this a friendship develops between them, but Bob proves to be a difficult man to know. And when Kirsty decides to make an offer for the inn and start a new life, it brings them into direct competition. Will they ever resolve their differences?

Books by Miranda Barnes
in the Linford Romance Library:

DAYS LIKE THESE

MIRANDA BARNES

A NEW BEGINNING

Complete and Unabridged

LINFORD
Leicester

First published in Great Britain in 2008

First Linford Edition
published 2009

British Library CIP Data

Barnes, Miranda.
  A new beginning- -
  (Linford romance library)
  1. Love stories.
  2. Large type books.
  I. Title II. Series
  823.9'2–dc22

  ISBN 978–1–84782–864–4

Published by
F. A. Thorpe (Publishing)
Anstey, Leicestershire

Set by Words & Graphics Ltd.
Anstey, Leicestershire
Printed and bound in Great Britain by
T. J. International Ltd., Padstow, Cornwall

This book is printed on acid-free paper

Back To The Past

Kirsty stopped the car on the brow of the hill and gazed with growing excitement at the view. Perfect. Exactly as she remembered it. Apart from the 'For Sale' sign flapping in the wind. She wondered what that was about.

Fells Inn. Ancient. Built of Lakeland stone. Painted white. The centrepiece of the hamlet, Fells. Behind it the lake, and then the mountainside, Goat Fell, sweeping up to the sky.

The sky, of course, was deep blue, like the lake. And the whole scene was bathed in brilliant spring sunshine. Just as it should be.

Kirsty smiled, reached for the ignition key, restarted the engine of her little VW Polo and began the long descent down the steep, winding lane to the lakeshore.

So far, so good.

★   ★   ★

The car park behind Fells Inn was a muddy morass dotted with shallow ponds. Winter rain on top of ground already waterlogged and churned up by the comings and goings of so many vehicles had taken its toll.

Kirsty took one look and reversed to park on the road at the front of the building. One thing she had not brought with her was a pair of wellies. Obviously a big mistake.

She took just one of her bags to start with and headed for the entrance to the inn.

She paused inside the front door and gazed around with growing pleasure. So she hadn't imagined it! Her memory hadn't played her false. It really was like this.

Blackened ceiling beams. Dark wood

panels on the walls. Gleaming brasses hung seemingly at random. Glass display cases dotted around, containing stuffed fish and preserved feathered creatures. An ancient stone-flagged floor, and chairs and tables almost as old. A log fire gently smouldering in the massive stone hearth.

No-one in sight, though.

She stood patiently at the bar, and after a minute or two a young man with a harassed look arrived. 'Yes?' he enquired. 'Can I help you?'

'Hello. I have a room reservation for the week. Kirsty Johnson.'

'Oh, right. I'll get one of the girls to come and see to you. Can I get you a drink? Cup of tea? Anything?'

She declined the offer. All she really wanted at this stage was to settle into her room and rest. It had been a long journey.

'I've been here before,' she said conversationally, 'but a long, long time ago.'

'That right? Well, wait there and I'll

just see who's here to get you booked in.'

He turned and disappeared through a doorway behind the bar. Kirsty felt slightly disappointed. It hadn't been much of a welcome. She shrugged. Oh well, she supposed the man was busy.

Yet she seemed to be the only customer.

Eventually a woman about her own age, mid-thirties, arrived and smiled brightly at Kirsty.

'Hello there! Sorry to keep you waiting. I'm Carol. How can I help?'

'I need booking in.'

Carol looked puzzled.

'The young man told me to wait here,' Kirsty said.

'Didn't he do it?' Carol asked.

Kirsty shook her head.

A small frown raced across Carol's face. 'Men!' she muttered.

Kirsty smiled.

Carol reached for the register. 'I hope you've not been waiting long?'

Kirsty shook her head. 'Only a minute or two.'

'Room Number Three,' Carol said. 'I don't know why Henry couldn't do this himself.'

'Henry?'

'The manager. The owner, actually. You just spoke to him.'

Kirsty gave Carol a sympathetic smile. She knew what managers could be like. Some of them were of the view that you didn't keep a dog and bark yourself.

★   ★   ★

'Right.' Carol closed the register, picked a key off a hook and turned to show Kirsty the way upstairs. 'We're quiet at the moment,' she said over her shoulder, 'so you've got a choice of rooms. If you don't like Number Three, I can show you one or two others.'

But the room was lovely. At least, it had a wonderful view of the lake, which was all Kirsty was really interested in.

5

'How beautiful,' she said with a sigh.

Carol smiled and stood back while Kirsty leaned out of the window and gazed across the shimmering water.

'Do you know,' she said, 'I believe I've had this room before. I came here once or twice as a little girl with my parents, and I'm sure this is the room I used to have.'

'Really?' Carol said. 'Fancy you remembering that.'

She glanced around and added, 'I don't suppose the room is any different. Even the wallpaper will probably be just the same.'

Kirsty looked round, noticed the wallpaper was a bit ragged and faded in places, and nodded her agreement. 'I think you're right.'

She caught Carol's eye and they both began to laugh.

'If the window rattles in the wind,' Carol advised, 'just jam a bit of folded paper between the cracks. These old sash windows leave a lot to be desired.'

'And if you get cold, there's spare

blankets in the wardrobe.'

'You've thought of everything,' Kirsty said smiling.

'You have to, to survive in a draughty old place like this.'

'The view's nice, though.'

Kirsty watched as a sudden rain squall moved across the placid surface of the lake.

'Oh, yes. The view's lovely,' Carol agreed. 'As long as it's not raining.'

★ ★ ★

By six-thirty Kirsty was ready for her evening meal. She made her way downstairs and settled at the end of the room, 'The Bar', where tables were set out for dining.

She studied the menu placed on her table. Judging by the greasy feel of the card, it had been in use a long time. The unadventurous list of contents tended to suggest the same thing.

She opted for the grilled salmon and made her way to the counter to order.

The man who had greeted her when she arrived was there, manning the bar. Henry, she remembered Carol had said his name was.

'Be with you in a minute,' he called.

She nodded and smiled, and watched as he unloaded glasses from a dishwasher. Obviously he didn't subscribe to the maxim that customers came first.

'Come on, Henry!' a man at the far end of the bar called. 'This is no way to run a business. You've got customers standing here, parched for a drink. And that young lady looks in need of nourishment.'

Henry reluctantly left the glasses. He gave Kirsty a weary smile and came to take her order. 'I'm working my fingers to the bone,' he complained, 'and do I get appreciated?'

'Is that why you're selling the place?' Kirsty asked him, remembering the 'For Sale' sign hanging outside the inn.

Henry nodded. 'One of the reasons. I've had enough here. Been here far too long.'

'How long?'

'All my life.'

'Really? You were born here?'

He nodded. 'Twenty-nine years ago. I made a promise to myself that I'd get out before I was thirty.'

'So it must have been your parents that had the place when I came here as a little girl.'

'Probably. Been in the family a long time. Anyway, settled in all right?'

'Yes, thanks. It's very . . . comfortable.'

He nodded without much interest and poured the glass of white wine Kirsty had requested to go with her meal.

As she returned to her table, Henry turned to attend to his other customer.

'The service here is non-existent,' she heard the customer, a big, burly man, complain to Henry. 'No wonder nobody comes in any more. No wonder the place has gone to the dogs.'

'Nobody comes in, Malcolm, because this place is at the back of beyond. It's the pits,' Henry said.

'Tourism's booming! There's more traffic than ever. The Lake District is so full you can hardly get in any more. There's hardly room for my sheep these days.'

'What more do you want?'

'This bit of the Lake District isn't like that,' Henry retorted. 'We're never full here. This valley is like the Australian Outback — empty.'

They talk like old sparring partners, Kirsty thought with amusement. Obviously well used to each other.

She felt a little sorry for Henry. It was a pity if the inn wasn't doing so well. She had wondered about that when she saw the 'For Sale' sign.

It really was a shame. She wouldn't want to see the place full all the time, with a queue of coaches at the door, but it was better for everybody when trade was good.

But already, she thought sadly, she had seen the signs that things were not going so well. Few customers. And the general run-down air of the place.

Faded and scruffy wallpaper in her room. Windows that needed replacing. Broken tiles in the bathroom.

Craig would have hated it here. He would have grimaced as soon as he came through the door and promptly turned round and gone elsewhere, somewhere more luxurious and inviting.

She smiled and thought what a good thing it was Craig wasn't here. He would just have spoiled it for her.

This was still a wonderful old place in a gorgeous setting, even if it wasn't as sparklingly well-kept as she remembered. It was in need of sprucing up, that was all. And some TLC. And a bit of money spending on it.

It was a long time since she had last stayed anywhere with unheated rooms, and she was sure she wasn't the only guest who would prefer her room to be en-suite.

These weren't luxuries any more.

People were used to such things these

11

days. They expected them.

Still, if business wasn't so good, Henry wouldn't be able to afford to have the work done. That was the end of it.

No good him having fancy aspirations he couldn't afford. No good at all.

That way led to Poverty Street, as her mother might have said. She smiled at the thought.

* * *

'Good evening.' She looked round and smiled again, this time at the tall, slim man taking his place at a nearby table.

'Take my advice,' he said to her. 'Be sure to sit well away from the door and wear two jumpers when you come in for a meal.

'It's always cold and draughty in here till someone gets round to livening up the fire.'

'Take no notice of him,' Carol called cheerfully from the other side of the room. 'Bob's always complaining about something.'

'And you always give me plenty to complain about,' the man rejoined.

'We're trying to persuade you to stay away, but you just don't take the hint,' Carol said with a grin.

Kirsty chuckled. 'You must know this place well?'

Bob nodded and looked grave for a moment, as though it were unfortunate but true.

'The food's not bad, though,' he added, as if in compensation, before opening a newspaper he had brought to the table with him.

Kirsty smiled again. She was doing a lot of that, she thought wryly. She must be enjoying herself.

Perhaps it had something to do with Craig not being here.

'Actually,' she said to Bob, 'there was a time when I knew this old place well, too. Or I thought I did. I used to come here as a little girl.'

'Before it went to pot? Before Henry

got his paws on it?'

She laughed. 'Oh, yes. It was lovely then. Always.'

'It is now, as well,' she added diplomatically.

Carol arrived from the kitchen with her meal.

By the time that was sorted out, Kirsty was disappointed to see that the man at the neighbouring table had disappeared.

Carol seemed surprised. 'Now where's Bob gone?' she murmured.

'He didn't say.'

Carol sighed.

'Oh, well, he must have changed his mind. Perhaps he's forgotten where he is and thinks we'll provide room service.'

Kirsty hoped it wasn't something she'd said that had made him leave.

'He doesn't like company,' Carol explained with a grimace, and added, 'which is probably why he comes here.'

'Am I the only guest?' Kirsty wanted to know.

14

'Apart from Bob, yes.'

'At the moment,' she added quickly. 'I hope you like it quiet?'

'Oh, I do.'

'You should get on very well with Bob, in that case.'

The next morning, Carol was serving breakfast. 'Are you never off duty?' Kirsty asked her.

'Not often, no,' Carol laughed. 'We're short of staff. I don't mind, though. We've got to keep the old place going. Besides, the money's handy.'

'Am I the only one for breakfast?'

'Just you and Bob. But he's had his.'

'Early bird, eh?'

'That's one name for him. Oh, don't get me wrong. He's all right, Bob, in his own way. We're used to him. He's always here.'

Kirsty was intrigued.

'Perhaps he doesn't have a home to go to?' she suggested.

'No,' Carol said without a smile. 'I don't believe he does now.'

A Friend In Need

After breakfast the next morning Kirsty set out to enjoy the spring sunshine. She strolled by the lake, along a rough path forged by sheep and countless walking boots.

In the woods, birch trees and hawthorn were coming into leaf.

No daffodils yet, though, Kirsty noted with a twinge of disappointment. Perhaps nobody had planted them in this part of the Lake District?

But the grass was a vibrant green, and already providing something tasty for the rabbits as well as the sheep.

And the sky was a wonderful blue again. Spring was most definitely here.

Oh, it was so beautiful!

She stopped and gave an involuntary pirouette. Then she laughed at herself.

How ridiculous she must look to anyone watching!

But she couldn't help it. She was so happy just to be here, to leave the office and the city behind for a few days.

And to leave Craig.

But she didn't want to think of him at the moment.

Thoughts of Craig were less pressing here, anyway.

She was glad of that, because at home they just wouldn't go away. Or, if they did, they had a way of returning when she wasn't ready for them. Then she was guaranteed another sleepless night to add to all the others.

But last night, here in The Fells Inn, she had slept soundly.

* * *

She strolled by the lake for a couple of hours, enjoying the views and the feel of the wind sweeping across the water. Then she called in at a café for a cup of tea and a sandwich.

She would have preferred to have brought a snack with her, but, disappointingly, Fells Inn had been unable to provide a packed lunch.

'Henry doesn't want us doing that,' a girl from the kitchen had said. 'He says it's not what he's paying us for. Sorry.'

Kirsty had been surprised, but she had tried not to let her disappointment show. It wasn't the girl's fault.

From now on, though, she decided, she would see what she could find in the little shop in the village. If nothing else, they ought to have apples and bananas, and chocolate bars and crisps. Bottles of water, too. She didn't need anything special.

On the way back, mid-afternoon, she heard the rattle of stones above her on the hill.

She looked up to see her fellow guest from the inn, Bob. He was sliding down a steep, stony section of path that was virtually a scree. And he was moving far faster than she would have cared to try.

She watched for a few moments until

he disappeared from view.

He looked at home on the slope, as if he knew what he was doing. He'd probably been up to the top, she thought with a pang of envy, wondering what it was like up there.

Well, she thought, now she had tried out her walking legs, maybe she could attempt something more adventurous tomorrow.

★ ★ ★

Back at the inn, Kirsty gratefully accepted the offer of a pot of tea from Carol.

'Had a nice day?' Carol asked.

'Lovely, thanks. I walked round the lake.'

'All the way? Goodness! It must be seven or eight miles.'

Kirsty felt pleased someone had recognised her achievement. 'Not bad for a townie, was it?' she said.

'Very good, I would say. I've lived here all my life, and I've never done it.

Or maybe I did once — when I was about eight years old.'

'The same for me,' Kirsty said with a laugh. 'That's when I last did it. I was with my dad.'

'But you can still do it. I don't think I could. Were there many people about?'

Kirsty shook her head. 'A few in the café at the far end of the lake, but I only passed four people walking.

'Oh, yes! And I caught a glimpse of Bob in the distance. On Goat Fell. High up.'

Carol chuckled and nodded. 'That would be him.'

'He's a real climber, is he?'

'I suppose he is, yes. A fell walker, anyway.'

'That will be why he's here such a lot. Where's he from?'

Carol shook her head.

'I don't really know. Somewhere in Lancashire or Yorkshire, I think. Some little place in that area.'

That covered a lot of territory, Kirsty

thought with amusement. Lancashire or Yorkshire.

'How about you?' Carol asked.

'Tyneside — Newcastle.'

'A Geordie, eh?'

'Through and through.'

'A real townie.'

Kirsty nodded. 'But I do like it here,' she added firmly. 'I like it a lot.'

★　★　★

A couple of days into her stay, Kirsty decided she was ready to be more adventurous. She had her eye on Goat Fell, the big mountain overlooking the village and the lake, which she had spotted Bob descending in a hurry.

It was a bright, sunny morning. The forecast was for showers later in the day, but there would be plenty of time before they arrived. Time enough, at least, for her to climb a little way up the mountain, maybe even to see the tarn half-way up.

Walking uphill was different to

21

walking on the flat around the lake, she soon discovered.

You got out of breath, for one thing — and very quickly. And the muscles in your legs soon began to hurt.

After a few minutes she stopped, shook her head and grinned ruefully. How unfit can one person allow herself to become?

She decided to go on. She knew already that she hadn't a hope of reaching the tarn, which was a good thousand feet above the lake, but she did want to climb a little higher.

The exercise would be good for her, she told herself.

It was hard work, though. More time had passed than she cared to remember since she had last done anything so strenuous.

I used to be so fit, too, she thought. Fitter than this, anyway. At school I even used to play hockey.

But it wasn't only the need for exercise and the memories of past athletic glories that drove her onwards and upwards.

Already the view was spectacular. The lake stretching away into the distance. The vivid green of the slopes on the other side of the valley. And in the far distance the tops of mountains a lot higher than Goat Fell.

She felt a growing excitement.

And she felt happy, too.

The cool air kissed her face. She could hear a breeze, higher up, whistling around the rocky crags.

A lamb called for its mother, and its mother's voice echoed back between the rocks.

She felt a long way from the city and didn't mind one little bit.

She was beginning to feel quite exhilarated.

Here and there, paths converged. Some were just sheep trails, winding across the fellside. Others bore the imprints of walking boots.

She alternated in taking them: a left here; a right fork there. But always heading slowly upwards, until at last, and to her surprise, she found herself on the shores of Goat Tarn.

It was a stunning little lake. More like a mirror than a body of water. She slowed when she saw it, overwhelmed by the beauty of the place and delighted by the knowledge that she had reached here unaided.

Tired and aching, maybe, but here. Definitely here.

She sat by the water's edge and slowly ate the chocolate bar, banana and apple she had brought with her.

Somehow the cheese sandwich she'd made didn't appeal. She left it in her pocket and took a sip from the water bottle she'd brought.

Suddenly, the lake was partly obscured by a puff of thin cloud, like mist, that swept quickly across from nowhere. Time to go, she thought, looking round. Perhaps the promised showers were not far away.

As she started downhill, she realised she had left it a little late.

The first of the showers had already arrived. Damp, moist cloud at least.

Then thin drizzle.

Her hair felt wet already. She smoothed it back and pulled up the hood of her jacket.

Not much of the valley could be seen now, and as she picked her way down the path, the rest of it disappeared surprisingly quickly.

She wasn't concerned. Just disappointed that the sunshine and the view had gone so soon.

The path was easy to follow at first. She moved down it confidently until she reached the second or third junction. Then . . . Had she taken the left or the right fork here?

It didn't matter. All routes led downhill.

Or so she thought, until the path she was on turned back uphill.

She stopped and frowned. She didn't remember this bit.

She turned round and could see nothing. Nothing at all.

She was surrounded by a blanket of cool, moist air.

Then it began to rain, and rain properly. Within minutes the water was sliding down the back of her neck and creeping up her sleeves and into her trainers. Her trousers stuck to her legs.

She still felt OK, though. Uncomfortable, but in control. And rational.

She didn't panic.

She remained calm, reasonably cheerful, even. But she knew that up here, simple discomfort could turn into something more serious. Hypochondria, for instance. No. That was wrong. What was it she was thinking of?

Hypothermia! That was it. How stupid she was.

She knew she had to get down out of the cooling rain while she was still strong and warm.

Easier said than done, though.

There was little wind but the rain grew heavier and wetter. It was no longer a light shower. More the onset of serious stuff fresh from the Atlantic.

And the cloud didn't lift. If anything, it grew thicker.

She walked down a little way, and then up again. Down some more. And all the time she sensed she was edging across the fellside.

That didn't feel right. Not at all.

She stopped. OK, let's think about this.

There was no way she should be on a path leading upwards.

She was supposed to be going down.

It should be straightforward.

She had come straight up; she should be able to go straight down.

She turned round and began heading back the way she had come.

Ten or fifteen minutes walking brought her back to a junction she recognised. It had her own fresh boot print on it.

This was where she had gone wrong. She'd turned left when she had come down from the tarn.

She should have kept straight on.

A long rattle of stones kept her stationary for a moment. She stood still, alarmed, and listened. More noises.

27

Alarm changed to a feeling of relief. Someone was coming down from the tarn. Thank goodness!

She waited. She heard the thud of heavy boots. Someone was moving fast.

A dark patch appeared, and grew. It became clearer.

She could make out a figure, looming ever larger. It spoke.

'This is no place to be just now, is it? I hope Carol's getting that fire lit for us.'

'Oh, Bob!' Kirsty breathed with nervous relief. 'What are you doing here?'

'Trying to get down before the rain arrives.'

'Well, you've failed. Just like me.'

'So it seems.' He reached her and stopped.

He smiled and eased the hood of his jacket back.

She was glad to see him. Glad to see anyone, but especially glad to see someone she knew. Sort of knew, anyway.

28

'How far have you been?' she asked.

He nodded over his shoulder. 'To the top.'

'Of Goat Fell?'

'Yes. You?'

'Oh, just to the tarn. I was feeling very pleased with myself for getting that far.'

'It's a stiff climb, especially if you're not used to it. Come on. This rain's getting heavier.'

It was, too, almost without her noticing. But she wasn't concerned now. She was pleased to be with a companion.

★ ★ ★

They set off, heading directly downhill.

I should have done this, Kirsty thought. I don't know why I wandered off to the side.

'I didn't see you up at the tarn,' Bob said over his shoulder.

'No. It's a little while since I was there, I suppose. I left just as the rain was starting.'

'That was an hour ago,' Bob exclaimed. He looked at her quizzically. 'You didn't get lost, did you?'

'Lost? Me?' She gave a little laugh. 'Of course not.'

He stopped and looked at her sternly. 'You got lost, didn't you?'

'Not exactly.'

'You got lost.'

'I always knew where I was,' she insisted. 'I just sort of . . . deviated. It wasn't the path I wanted.

'But I was always on a path,' she added defensively.

Bob smiled and started walking again.

'It's easy done,' he said. 'Once the cloud comes in it's easy to get disorientated. You think up is down, right is left.'

'You probably wandered across the fellside on a sheep track.'

'Yes,' she admitted. 'I think I probably did.

'I'd just come back to where I'd started when I heard you coming.'

30

'You didn't seem to have any doubts about where you were, though.'

He didn't now either, she thought, as he plunged on down the path.

'I know this mountain like the back of my hand,' Bob told her. 'I ought to, the times I've climbed it.'

'It's your favourite?'

'Seems to be.'

They hit some steep screes.

Conversation became difficult. They had to concentrate on their footing.

They didn't really speak again until they were at the bottom of the hill and crossing the field towards the inn.

'I enjoyed that,' Kirsty said.

'Getting cold and wet and lost?'

'Being up there. Under my own steam. Feeling the wind and the rain.'

'You'll likely be sore tomorrow,' Bob suggested with a grin.

'I'm sure I shall be.

'It's a long time since I've had such an energetic day.'

'You've done well, in that case.'

He said it as if he meant it, and for

the first time in a long while, Kirsty felt quite proud of herself.

'You need some proper boots, though,' Bob said, glancing down at her sodden trainers as she squelched through the mud.

'I wouldn't try climbing again in them.'

Even that little reprimand didn't take the shine off the day.

She smiled at Bob.

'I know,' she said with a grimace. 'Don't think I haven't noticed my feet are in danger of becoming webbed!'

He grinned back and they forged on in a companionable silence, heading for the comfort of Fells Inn, a roof over their heads and a roaring fire.

Food For Thought

Kirsty had much to think about over supper, which was just as well, as she was entirely alone. There was no sign at all of Bob, who was still the only other guest.

She knew she needed some better clothing if she was to do any more walking in the mountains.

Proper boots would have to be the priority, but she also needed a jacket that did a better job of keeping out the rain than the thin cagoule she had brought with her.

She needed better trousers, too. The jeans she had worn on Goat Fell were so wet they would take the rest of the week to dry. Besides, they had chafed her legs.

She could do with a little backpack,

too. You couldn't stuff everything you needed into your pockets.

This was quite a list she was compiling. Would it be worth it, spending money on all those things? Would she get enough use out of them?

She shook her head impatiently. It certainly would be worth it. She would make sure of that.

* * *

Despite feeling stiff and tired, she had enjoyed her little adventure. It had been exciting, and had made her feel good about herself. Better, anyway. Even if she did feel tired now, it was a healthy fatigue. Muscles well-used, especially the ones she had forgotten about. Face glowing.

Besides, she had a goal now, a target. She wanted to reach the summit of Goat Fell.

Maybe not this week, but sometime — and soon.

You met such nice people on the mountains, that was another thing. Like? Well, like the handful she had exchanged greetings with on her walks. And like Bob.

People here at the inn, as well. Carol, for instance. But Bob, especially.

The mysterious Mr Bob. At first sight he seemed pretty remote, aloof even. You certainly wouldn't call him sociable. He kept himself to himself.

But he was a different person if you encountered him outdoors, as Kirsty had done. He seemed more at ease there. More comfortable, somehow. Friendlier.

Happier even.

She felt she could just about understand that.

Her own brief experience on Goat Fell had given her a sense of being almost a different person, a better, stronger person.

Out on the mountains you were being challenged by the terrain and the weather, and how you responded said something about what sort of person you were.

If you did well, you knew it. You could be proud of yourself. And you didn't need anyone to tell you.

She smiled at the memory of Bob appearing so unexpectedly out of the cloud.

He'd been so tough and capable. And good-humoured. Not handsome, though, she thought with a wry grin. Definitely not handsome.

Well . . . slightly handsome, perhaps, in a rugged, outdoor sort of way.

She couldn't imagine him setting female hearts a-flutter in the city, in a cocktail bar, say, or in an office. But up there on Goat Fell he'd been in his element, and he'd been transformed.

Perhaps he really was happier in the mountains?

Or maybe he was someone who found what most people regarded as 'normal life' dull?

It was hard to tell at the moment which camp he fell into.

★ ★ ★

The crash of things falling in the kitchen interrupted Kirsty's thoughts. She heard Henry complaining loudly. She heard Carol — poor Carol! — trying unsuccessfully to placate him. It was a wonder she stayed here. It really was.

'I hope that wasn't my meal ending up on the floor?' she said with a grin, when Carol eventually appeared in the dining room.

Carol raised her eyes towards the ceiling. 'He says we're going to bankrupt him, the way we're all going on.'

Fat chance! Kirsty thought, as Carol hurried back to the kitchen. Henry must be nearly there already, all by himself. All by his own efforts. Or lack of them.

Why couldn't he do things differently? Or even just put a bit more thought and effort into what he did do?

Laziness or lack of interest?

The latter, probably.

From what she'd seen and heard, Henry just didn't want to be here.

There was a lot you could do with the old place, though. Even she could see that.

But the first thing the Inn needed was more customers.

The money they brought in would finance the maintenance and improvements the building required.

Getting them would be a challenge, of course, but you could always start gradually, doing little things. You didn't have to start by spending a lot of money upfront.

'Does it hurt a lot?'

She looked up and gave an embarrassed little laugh. 'Hello, Bob. I didn't notice you come in.'

'Silent as a shadow. That's me.'

'Not this afternoon, you weren't. I heard you clattering down the mountain long before I saw you.'

'I was in a hurry. Didn't want to get wet.'

'So how are the aches and bruises, and the blisters?'

'Surprisingly, not too bad. I'm a bit tired, but otherwise I'm fine. It was a good day, wasn't it? And now I'm just sitting here, thinking.'

'About what? It looked painful.'

She hesitated. 'Won't you sit down? Have you eaten?'

'Not yet, no,' he admitted.

He looked around indecisively, and then back at Kirsty. 'Would company bother you?'

'Not at all. Sit down, please.'

He did, placing the pint of beer he'd brought with him on the table. 'So what were you thinking?' he asked.

'I was actually wondering what someone could do to make this place more popular and more profitable. Poor Carol. Henry's blaming her for his impending bankruptcy.'

Bob smiled. 'Oh, that's a long-running story. Henry wants out, basically. He's not interested in doing anything to improve things. So the old place continues its long slide into ruination.'

He looked at Kirsty thoughtfully. 'What would you do to improve it?'

'Well, first I would do something about the car park. Drain it, or something. Make it possible for people to use it without wearing thigh waders.'

'Put some field drains in and a load of hard-core,' Bob said. 'Next?'

'I'd get some young lad to design a website. It wouldn't have to be anything fancy. Just a website that would allow people to find Fells Inn on the internet.'

Bob nodded. 'They certainly need more customers.'

'I would employ a couple more staff like Carol,' Kirsty went on, 'people who would enjoy being here, who would work hard and make guests feel welcome when they arrived.

'And I would see my bank manager about a loan to allow me to put in central heating and en-suite facilities. I know those alterations would be costly, but I bet they would soon pay their way.'

She paused, smiled and added, 'That would be for starters. Oh, and I would provide packed lunches for guests.'

'I can see you've thought about this a lot,' Bob said, nodding with apparent approval.

She laughed. 'It doesn't take a genius.'

'You're right. Just someone with the interest, and a bit of get-up-and-go.'

'Well, that'd my contribution. What would you do, Bob? You're here a lot, Carol says. So you must know what's wrong with the place.'

He smiled and shook his head. 'It's no good asking me. I don't know about these things. I'm just a paying guest who likes the place, with all its faults.'

'Come on, Bob. There must be something you would change.'

'Well . . . a different beer, for a start. I'm not very fond of this one.'

'Bob!'

★   ★   ★

41

Kirsty woke up during the night and thought of something else to tell Bob. Rattling windows. She lay for a while and listened to hers.

A bit of a wind had got up. She could hear it lashing the old sycamore trees. It was raining again, too, splattering against the window. Goat Fell would be out of the question tomorrow. She could visualise it now under a thick black cap of heavy, wet cloud.

She shivered and slipped back into a kindly sleep.

As she dressed the next morning, she added other items to her mental list of things to tell Bob.

But, disappointingly, he wasn't there for breakfast.

'Bob already had his?' she asked Carol, hoping he hadn't.

'Yes,' Carol replied. 'He's away now.'

Kirsty glanced out of the window. 'Surely he's not out walking in this weather?'

'Oh, no. He's away home.'

'Home?'

Kirsty felt doubly disappointed. Not only would she not be able to resume her conversation with Bob, but he'd left without telling her. Without saying goodbye. What a strange man he was.

'Is there anything else I can get you?' Carol asked.

Kirsty shook her head. 'No, thanks. I'll get a move on.'

'You're not thinking of walking yourself, are you?'

'Not today. Today I'm going shopping.'

'Oh?' Carol looked interested. 'Shopping? That's more like it.'

'I'm going to look for some outdoor trousers and a better jacket. And some boots. One or two other things, as well. A backpack maybe.

'Where would you recommend I go?'

'Keswick. There are plenty of outdoor shops there. And at this time of year, some are bound to have sales on.'

'Right. Keswick, then. That's where I'll go.'

She added, as an afterthought, 'Did

Bob say where he was going? Where he lives, I mean?'

Carol shook her head. 'I never even saw him. He was too early for me.'

Man of Mystery! Kirsty thought with a wry smile. Gone into the night. Well, the early morning, at least. Pity.

'That's what he's like,' Carol went on. 'Comes and goes, goes and comes. He's a law unto himself. All you really know about Bob is that he'll appear again before very long.'

Time Will Tell

Keswick was quiet. That was more to do with the weather than the time of year, Kirsty suspected. Incessant rain, falling in a steady downpour, had a way of emptying streets.

She spent a pleasant couple of hours browsing in some of the many shops which catered for the outdoor trade, and then retreated to Sophie's Kitchen for an early lunch.

Sophie turned out to be plump and friendly, and eager to dispense good advice.

'Keep off the fells, I tell them,' she said to Kirsty. 'What's wrong with down here? I say. Mountains are all very well to look at, but being on them is unpleasant and dangerous. You can get wet. You can get cold. You can get injured. And even on a perfect day, climbing mountains can tire you out.'

'Exhaust you, even?' Kirsty suggested cheerfully.

'Exactly! What's wrong with staying in the valley, and just looking at them?'

'Nothing?' Kirsty ventured.

'Nothing. Right. So you've been shopping?' Sophie said, spying Kirsty's carrier bags. 'What have you been buying?'

'Boots. Backpack. A new jacket for the mountains.'

Sophie shook her head. 'Don't say you haven't been warned.'

Kirsty was in the middle of eating her panini when Craig rang.

'How's it going?'

'Fine, thanks, Craig. How are you?'

'OK. I was just worried about you.'

'Worried? Craig, when did you ever worry about me?'

He chuckled. 'So everything's all right? Enjoying yourself?'

'I am, actually, yes. It's a beautiful place.'

'That's good. Not a bit isolated?'

'It is, yes. But isn't that the whole point?'

'She knew what he really meant. He meant, was she missing him? Did she think they should reconsider?'

But it was true he would be worried about her. She knew that. Craig was kind and considerate. A good man.

People had been telling her that for longer than she could remember.

'Craig,' she said gently now, 'we were going nowhere, you and I. We were right to call it a day. And you needn't worry about me. It's very nice of you, but I'm fine.'

'Sure?'

'Certain,' she said, with tears not far away.

He sounded relieved. She could imagine his face, how he would worry. Now a worry lifted. All smiles again.

'We did the right thing, Craig,' she repeated softly.

There was a bit more, then the conversation ended, died really, and she rang off.

She hadn't been entirely sure about Craig before she came on this break, but she was now. They had done the right thing.

'Man trouble?' the redoubtable Sophie asked.

Kirsty smiled. 'Well, yes. You could say that. He's worried about me, he says.'

'Guilty conscience,' Sophie said with a sniff. 'Men! You can't tell me what they're like. Been married three times. All of them a mistake. Never happier than now.'

'Single and successful businesswoman?'

'You bet! I've put the Atlantic between me and my mistakes, and made a success of my life.'

* * *

As she went back to her car, Kirsty thought about her own life.

For several years, she had believed she and Craig would marry, set up house together and have a family. She had assumed her life with him would be like her parents' life together had been. Herself and Craig. Together. Forever. Till Death did them part.

But somewhere along the way all that had changed.

She couldn't remember why, or when, or even how. She really didn't know how it had happened, but it had.

Slowly, steadily, the questions had arisen. Nothing had happened specifically. Time had just drifted by, and with it the realisation that perhaps it wasn't going to happen. Marriage and children, and all that. Not with Craig, anyway.

It wasn't just her that had come to feel that way, either. She had seen, and understood instinctively, that Craig had felt the same.

So they had agreed to step back from their relationship.

But even that had not been clear-cut. Several weeks had drifted by. A couple of months of occasional contact. Then she had decided to come here and have a break, with some misgivings, it had to be said.

Yet . . . and yet . . . she thought, until he rang, she hadn't thought of Craig all week. Surely that meant something?

Well, what did it mean? Not much, probably. It didn't mean she and Craig were over altogether, for instance. All it probably meant was that they had both been busy and thinking of other things.

It didn't mean they were definitely not going to be together for the rest of their lives, did it? Well, no. Perhaps not.

But it probably did.

Oh, how complicated everything was!

Kirsty started the engine and put the car in gear.

They would just have to wait and see.

Perhaps time would tell.

Back To Work

'Good holiday, Kirsty?' Emma smiled. 'You look as if you enjoyed it. Doesn't she?' she added, turning to the office at large.

There was general support for the proposition, except from young Jason. 'I don't rate her tan,' he said.

'She's been to the Lake District, Jason,' Emma pointed out. 'You don't go there for a sun tan.'

'What's the point, then?' Jason persisted, with a wink at Kirsty. 'She could have stopped at home, and saved a lot of money. Pubs any good?' he added as an afterthought.

'The one I stayed in was very nice. Quiet and olde-worlde.'

'Quiet? No decent music, then?'

'None at all.'

'Honestly!' Emma interjected. 'Is that all you want out of a holiday, Jason, sunshine, beer and music?'

'Yeah.' Jason thought about it a moment more before he added, 'and girls.'

'There weren't any girls either,' Kirsty said. 'Just people my age — and not many of them.'

Jason pulled a face that spoke volumes.

Fortunately, Emma's phone rang just then, as did Jason's a moment later. Anna and David, the other members of the team, got back to work. As did Kirsty, still smiling from the exchanges with Jason.

They were a good bunch, she thought fondly. It was lovely to see them all again. It was nice to be back, in fact. Sort of. In a way.

She sighed and looked to see what was in her in-tray.

It was a busy office. The team was part of a wholesale business that imported furniture.

Rustic oak tables and chairs from France. Ornate mirrors from Italy. Fine leather upholstery from Spain. And, increasingly, shopfuls of all kinds of stuff from China. Far from being a distant, unknown land, China seemed now to be the place where nearly everything you bought was made.

Especially furniture, Kirsty thought, as she processed yet another invoice.

Already, after just a couple of hours back in the office, she felt exhausted by the torrent of paperwork. In fact, she felt as if she'd never been away.

Later, over a cup of coffee, she gathered her thoughts. She would have to do a bit of shopping at lunch-time. There was very little food in the house. But maybe she could leave it until after work? She could call at the supermarket on the way home. Perhaps have a pizza, as well?

Her friend, Joyce, might like to join her. She could give her a ring. Find out.

Then she wondered whether to ring

Craig. It seemed strange to have been back in Newcastle for a whole twenty-four hours and not to have contacted him.

Her hand closed on the phone. She picked it up, hesitated and rang Joyce.

'First day back, huh?' Joyce said, when they met up later.

Kirsty nodded and sipped her glass of allegedly health-giving tropical-mix fruit juice.

'How was it?'

'Lovely, Joyce. Super. Wonderful.'

They looked at each other and began to laugh.

'Work, I meant!' Joyce said.

'I know you did.'

Kirsty pulled a face. 'Oh, the job's fine, I suppose. And they're a good crew to I work with. I've been there two years now, which is as long as I've been anywhere. So it must be OK.'

'But?'

'Oh, you know how it is, Joyce. I had a lovely holiday, and I'm feeling a bit out of sorts now. I wish I was still there.'

'The Lakes in April? What was the weather like?'

'Not bad. There was a bit of rain.' She hesitated and then added, 'Quite a lot, actually.'

'That's why they have lakes. Did nobody tell you?'

Kirsty pulled another face. 'It wasn't that much, really. Besides, it was mostly on the mountains. It was usually fine when you got down in the valley.'

'On the mountains? What on earth were you doing on the mountains?'

'Walking, of course.'

'You? Walking?'

'It's the new me,' Kirsty said with a grin. 'I like walking. It's good for you, and enjoyable. You see things,' she added vaguely. 'Views, and such.'

'Do you?' Joyce looked unconvinced. 'What does Craig think about this new enthusiasm? Does he approve?'

'It's nothing to do with Craig what I do.'

Joyce waited expectantly. She looked as if she was holding her breath.

Kirsty sighed. She hadn't said anything to Joyce about what she and Craig had decided. Or to anyone else, for that matter. But she supposed there had to be a first time. She would have to start telling people sometime.

'Joyce, Craig and I are not really together any more.'

'What does that mean? You've split up?'

'No, nothing like that. Well . . . yes, it does mean it's over, I suppose. We're still friends, but . . . '

'But there's going to be no church bells? And no little Craigs?'

Kirsty smiled reluctantly. 'That's about it. At least, I don't think so. Well, there might be. It's not as if . . . Oh, I don't know, Joyce!'

Joyce squeezed her friend's hand sympathetically. 'You don't sound very sure, Kirsty.'

'Well, what can I say? Things haven't been so good between us. Nothing dramatic. But . . . I suppose the truth is that we've grown apart. We're still friends, but that's as much as we want to be now.'

'So you haven't actually finished with each other?'

'Well . . . '

'So there's still a chance, then?'

'Oh, Joyce! You're always trying to get me married off. Just because you and Alan . . . '

'It's about time, Kirsty, don't you think?'

She did, actually.

On the way home that was what she did think about.

It was true. She wasn't getting any younger. The infamous biological clock was ticking. She could hear it. And it was getting louder.

She did want a family. And a husband she loved, and who loved her. She did.

But was it going to be Craig? She wished she knew for sure.

Sometimes she thought: of course it is. Then she had these uncertainties, these questions, just as Craig seemed to have.

57

On the other hand, they both had a lot invested in this relationship. They couldn't just give up on it, could they? Oh, how she wished she knew.

★ ★ ★

Kirsty met up with Joyce again a couple of evenings later, when they went for their regular swim. Joyce set off briskly on her routine quarter-mile of freestyle. Kirsty could never keep up with her, and this time felt even less inclined than usual to try.

She swam four lengths of breast-stroke, two of backstroke and two of what passed with her as freestyle. Then she retired to the sauna and waited for Joyce to join her.

She felt vaguely dissatisfied. Disappointed even. She should have felt so much better after her holiday, but she didn't. In fact, she wished she could return to last week and have her holiday all over again.

She wondered how they were all

getting on at Fells Inn without her, and if the mountains were still so green and the lake so blue and mysterious.

Carol would still be there, of course. And Henry, presumably, if he hadn't sold the place. Maybe Bob, too.

She sighed.

Another consideration was her house. While she'd been away, it had been possible to forget about it, but since she'd been back, she had remembered. Vividly.

It wanted so much doing to it. Nearly everything, in fact.

And what didn't want doing wanted replacing. Carpets, curtains, décor. Even the furniture. But she didn't have the energy or the interest, not to mention the money.

Then there was her parents' house, which she had inherited a couple of years' earlier when her mother had passed away.

She still hadn't been able to get rid of it, or decide what to do with it. Too many memories.

She needed to move on, but she hadn't the energy.

Maybe it would be easier when she and Craig finally decided where their relationship was going.

If indeed it was going anywhere.

* * *

The door of the sauna creaked open. Joyce appeared, looking red-faced and healthy. 'That was good. I needed some exercise. I didn't come last week, with you being away.'

'Missed me, huh?'

'I did, yes.'

They smiled at one another.

'Alan was most put out when you were away,' Joyce said. 'He said it meant he couldn't go for his usual night out with the lads. He couldn't leave me on my own.

'I had to practically push him out the door.

'I do need at least one night a week to myself.'

'It was good of him to think of you like that,' Kirsty said. 'Especially after all these years together. You're lucky.'

'Lucky? Me? Having Alan cluttering up the house with his golf clubs and his computers?'

Kirsty smiled.

'You're right, though,' Joyce admitted. 'I know I am lucky.'

And Kirsty knew it was true.

Sometimes she quite envied Joyce. Good husband, nice home, a job she liked as a receptionist at an optician's.

She almost had it all. Everything you needed to be happy. If only they could have the child she and Alan both wanted and longed for, Joyce's life really would be complete.

'So,' Joyce said now. 'Feeling better today? Got over the holiday blues?'

'No, actually. Not at all.'

Joyce arranged herself on the wooden slats of the sauna seat and flicked water at the hot stones. There was a hiss and a small cloud of steam puffed up towards the ceiling.

'So?' she said. 'What's the problem?'

'Oh, Joyce, I don't have a problem! It's not like that.'

'Well, what is it like?'

Kirsty leaned back.

'I just feel a bit flat, that's all,' she said. 'I had a lovely time in the Lakes. It was so beautiful there. Lovely, too, at the inn where I stayed. And then I've come back to . . . this.

'A job that's all right in some ways, but is basically pretty boring. A cold, empty house. On my own. Nothing to look forward to.'

'Wow! That's more than post-holiday blues, girl. That's a full-blown life crisis.'

'No, it's not. Don't be silly.'

'You have a good job and a decent home, Kirsty. Your mum's house, as well. You're very lucky.'

'Mum's house is part of the problem, Joyce. I don't know what to do with it. And I'm not thrilled about mine, either.

'I don't want to be there any more. Not alone.'

'Craig?'

'Well, the plan was to sell the two houses and his flat, and for us both to live somewhere new. I don't know what's going to happen now.'

Tactfully, Joyce didn't ask again about marriage plans. Instead, she said, 'Any plans for tonight?'

Kirsty shook her head.

'Fancy getting a DVD? 'Miss Potter' is supposed to be good.'

'Is that . . . ?'

'It's about the children's author, yes. And, yes, it's set in the Lake District,' Joyce added with a grin.

'That's a lovely idea, Joyce,' Kirsty said with enthusiasm. 'Let's go.'

An Excellent Suggestion

The film was lovely, apart from Miss Potter's publisher fiancé perishing seemingly of a bad cough before she could get him to the altar.

Miss Potter did wonderfully well, picking herself up from one mishap after another to emerge as a phenomenally successful children's author.

After the sadness of losing her fiancé, she took herself off to live in the Lake District, which in the film was so dreamily beautiful it made Kirsty wish all over again that she was on holiday still.

'What a rotten life,' Joyce said afterwards. 'Can you imagine? That big house in London, that fabulously rich family with its cotton mills in the north, servants everywhere, a great social life, and what does she do? She takes herself off to this half-derelict farmhouse, probably damp and riddled with wood-worm, and sits writing stories about bunny rabbits. And gets even richer!'

'Terrible,' Kirsty agreed.

'I mean,' Joyce went on, 'how was she ever going to meet an eligible young man in a place like that?'

'Not easily. But she did, didn't she? Eventually.'

'Well . . . Not really. He was her childhood sweetheart, after all, wasn't he?'

'He wasn't really eligible, not in the sense her mother meant. I mean, he worked for a living!'

'But she no longer had to marry a man-about-town with good prospects. She was free at last to marry a countryman, someone just like her at heart,' Kirsty pointed out.

'That's all very well, but I don't know what her mother must have thought. Anyway, all those gloomy mountains, and all that rain.'

Joyce stopped and stared with suspicion at Kirsty, who was laughing and shaking her head.

'You're going to tell me again how lovely it is there, aren't you?'

Kirsty nodded.

'You should go back,' Joyce said. 'Have another holiday.'

'Why don't you?'

'I just might,' Kirsty said.

Joyce stared hard at her.

'Now wait a minute,' she said slowly, 'you gave me to understand the inn was a bit of a dump, and it never stopped raining.

'So why would you even consider going there again?'

'Well . . . '

'So what, actually, is the attraction, Kirsty? No, don't tell me. Craig isn't going. So . . . ' Her eyes lit up. 'You've met someone else, haven't you?'

'Of course not!' Kirsty laughed now with embarrassment.

'No? Was there no-one else there at all?'

'Men, you mean? Well, there was Henry, the owner, who's nice enough, but basically pretty useless.

'And there was one male guest.'

'Ah! Tell me more.'

Kirsty went on to tell her about Bob.

Joyce heard her out and then sighed. 'Not terribly promising, is he?

'Mind you, maybe you gave up too soon? He might be interesting if you got to know him better.

'And maybe if you did go back, he might be there again. What do you think?'

'I have no idea.'

★　★　★

The conversation with Joyce wouldn't leave her mind. That night in bed, Kirtsy found herself turning it over and over. Not the bit about Bob, of course. That was far too silly. Joyce had just been teasing her, as usual.

No, it was all the stuff about the Lake District and Beatrix Potter that ran around her head half the night.

She could see the towering mountainsides in her mind's eye. And the lake, as a squall hit the far shore.

The sound of the brooks tinkling into the streams. The noise of the rushing river, before it tumbled into the lake.

She could hear sheep bleating on the hills and the rush of the wind in the sycamores near Fells Inn. And the clatter of pots being dropped in the kitchen. Poor Carol.

She smiled as she snuggled deeper under her quilt. Why shouldn't she go back? No reason at all. She still had some holiday to take. She'd go. She would.

Apart from anything else, she had unfinished business with Goat Fell. She wanted to stand on the summit. Maybe she would do it on a day when Bob could see her. That would impress him.

One fantasy led to another.

Soon she was thinking of Fells Inn again, and how she could improve it, given the chance.

She would make it more welcoming, for a start.

One way would be to do some landscaping around the building. Native shrubs and small trees. Flowers in tubs in summer. Climbing plants on the front wall. Roses, probably.

She wondered briefly what they would all think of it.

Henry probably wouldn't care. Carol would like it, though. And Bob? What would Bob think?

* * *

The next day was difficult, all the way through. For a start, she had woken up with a headache. Not enough sleep, she supposed. Then e-mails, faxes and phone calls ran her off her feet from the moment she arrived in the office.

French tables and chairs, in oak, had not arrived at the store that had ordered them. Instead, they had been delivered to some company in South-port that now wanted to know why.

A French lorry driver who couldn't read English, or was in a hurry to get home, was her best guess.

It was sheer luck that the stuff had reached England at all.

Then Philip at the warehouse wasn't very happy about a consignment of Chinese mirrors that had been cracked in transit.

The insurance company wasn't happy, either. Pay-bills, in the Accounts Department, wanted to know if they should pay for them or hang on until the insurance claim was sorted.

The morning raced by.

Craig rang, but Kirsty had little time to speak to him. Yes, she would have a meal with him the next evening. Yes, they had things to discuss.

After lunch, she wished she had not eaten anything. Her stomach was in turmoil. By mid-afternoon she wondered if she was coming down with something. By five she was sure of it.

By seven she was shivering at home under an extra quilt, feeling as if her head was going to explode.

She was cold. Or was she warm? She couldn't tell.

All she knew was that she had a right dose of something not very nice.

She was off work three days. Then, still feeling semi-wretched, she dragged herself back. Somehow she coped. She managed.

She did what had to be done, and began to look forward to feeling well again. But it didn't happen.

The next week she saw her doctor.

'Rest, my dear,' Dr Gregg said in his lovely Scottish accent. 'That's all you need.'

She stared at him, reluctant to accept so simple a cure.

'The virus has done its best, or its worst,' he explained. 'It can do no more. You're over it. I can see how poorly you feel still, but recovery takes time.'

She nodded. 'I do feel poorly. You're right.'

'I was hoping for some antibiotics, or

something,' she added vaguely.

'They wouldn't help, I'm afraid. And we don't give them out unless they would.'

'Some people,' he added with a conspiratorial smile, 'would have us give them out like sweeties.'

She knew what he meant. She'd read about that.

'Any chance of you getting away for a few days?' Dr Gregg asked.

'Away where? What do you mean?' She was momentarily non-plussed.

'Personally, I would always recommend Scotland, but you might prefer somewhere a little warmer and less windy at this time of year. It's worth thinking about.'

On the way home she did think about it. And when she arrived home she checked her diary and her bank balance.

Then she smiled.

There was only one place she wanted to go.

Return to Fells Inn

She couldn't put off seeing Craig any longer. They met for lunch in a restaurant near the Quayside that she didn't know. It was a lot posher than their usual lunchtime venues, but Craig had insisted it was his treat. He got to his feet as she approached his table.

'Good to see you up and about again, Kirsty,' he said with a smile. 'Feeling better?'

'Yes, thanks. I'm over the worst of it now.'

'That's good.'

He was immaculately dressed, as usual. Smart navy suit. Pristine white shirt. Fashionably flamboyant tie.

Black brogues you would have been able to see your face in if it hadn't been for the pattern in the leather.

Craig was already a successful young solicitor. And just the sight of him made Kirsty feel twenty years older.

He got her comfortably seated and then turned his attention to the menu. 'The soups are good here,' he murmured. 'And the fish.'

'Craig . . . '

'Especially the red snapper. I love that.'

'Craig?'

He raised a questioning eye from the menu.

'Craig, I'm not terribly hungry, to be honest.

'I've only got forty minutes anyway. We're very busy.'

'Nonsense. You've got to eat. You're recovering your strength.'

She compromised. She had a bowl of carrot and coriander soup accompanied by a roll fresh from the oven. Craig was disappointed, but he had the sense to let it go.

'What are we going to do, Craig?' Kirsty began. 'What is it you want to do?'

'That depends on you, old thing.'

'For goodness sake!' she snapped.

His raised eyebrows stopped her saying something she might have regretted later.

'Well,' she said carefully, 'as I said before, I think we were right to call time, Craig. Our relationship just wasn't working for me any more. I'd felt that for some time, and after the last few weeks I'm certain of it.

'I'm sorry,' she added.

After the briefest of pauses, Craig said, 'But we can still be friends, can't we?'

She nodded. She felt very sad. Guilty, as well. But better to have said what she'd just said now, than to have had to stay it a few years down the line, when parting would have been so much more difficult in every way.

On her way back to the office, Kirsty wondered if Craig would meet someone else. She hoped so. She really did hope so.

All that time, though, she thought

sadly. All that time wasted. And Joyce was right. She wasn't getting any younger.

But at least they could both get on with their lives now. That was something.

Fells Inn looked just the same. She stopped at the top of the little hill overlooking it for a moment to satisfy herself on that point, and then swept down the lane to park outside. Exactly the same, she thought with pleasure.

Even the 'For Sale' board was still in place.

'You're back!' Carol cried, as she walked through the door.

'Can't keep me away.'

'It's good to see you again, Kirsty.'

'Thank you, Carol. It's lovely to be here again.'

Carol handed her a key. 'It's the same room as last time. That OK?'

'Perfect. I'll get settled in. Then I'll come and have a pot of tea with you.'

'I'll be here.'

Even the view from the window was

the same. No Bob, though, Kirsty thought with disappointment.

She had seen a man coming out of another room and had been about to call a greeting, until she realised Bob couldn't possibly have put on so much weight in the short time since she'd last seen him.

Nor could he have become less tall.

Besides, he wouldn't have been wearing a business suit, she thought with a smile. That would have looked quite wrong on him.

'Not a bad day,' the man had said as he passed by.

'Beautiful,' she had replied with an automatic smile.

A sales rep, probably, she thought, a man who would always have easy words for people. Not at all like Bob.

But she had other things to think about now, things she hadn't been able to think about at home.

First, how did she really feel about Fells Inn now she was here once again? The same, she decided. Exactly the same.

She loved it. Even though it was shabby and neglected, she loved it. She always had.

All it needed was someone to care for it, someone with a bit of money and energy. Given someone like that, it could be as perfect again as it had been all those years ago. Even more perfect, in fact.

Surely there must be someone who could meet the challenge?

* * *

Carol brought a pot of tea into the dining room, and joined Kirsty.

'Much been happening?' Kirsty asked.

Carol shook her head. 'Just the usual. We've had our regular over-nighters, and the locals in the bar. Pretty quiet, really.'

'Regulars? Who stays here regularly?'

'People on business. Medical reps. Salesmen. I don't know exactly.'

That was interesting. So there was a regular trade, Kirsty thought. Not just people on holiday and people passing through, but people who returned because they liked it or it suited them. You could build on that.

'Why would they come out here, rather than stay in the town?' she asked Carol.

'We're cheaper, I expect. And some people like peace and quiet. There's always plenty of that here.'

'Where's Henry?' Kirsty wanted to know.

'It's his day off. He goes into town and stays overnight. Stops with friends somewhere. Rumour has it,' Carol said, 'there's a woman in his life. Can you believe that?'

Not easily, Kirsty thought. But for every Jack there was a Jill. Wasn't that what they used to say?

'But he is coming back?' she pressed. 'He hasn't sold the place?'

'Sold it?' Carol chuckled. 'Chance would be a fine thing. I wish he would, though. I really do.

'I wish someone would come along

who actually wanted to be here. I'm sick of Henry's moaning. It's as if the place is a millstone round his neck. He doesn't know how lucky he is.'

'It would need someone with a lot of money,' Kirsty ventured.

'Not really. You could buy Fells Inn for what you would pay for a house around here. Mind, you'd need money to put it to rights.' Carol shrugged and added, 'but you could just stick it on the mortgage, I suppose.'

The conversation meandered in other directions and then came back to visitors, of whom there had been few since Kirsty's last visit.

'What about that man who was here last time? Bob?' she said casually.

'Haven't seen him for a week or two.'

Kirsty felt disappointed.

'But he's coming tomorrow night,' Carol added.

A Decision Is Made

Kirsty saw him arrive in the dining area a couple of mornings later. 'So it's true!' she said to him. 'You really are here all the time.'

'Hello there. Back again?'

'I believe I am, yes.'

He returned her smile, but it was a bit of a grudging effort. He didn't seem exactly overjoyed to see her.

'Breakfast, Bob?' Carol asked.

'No, thanks. I'm just on my way out.'

'You won't get far on an empty stomach,' Carol told him.

He didn't reply and gave Kirsty a nod as he headed for the door.

'Mr Cheerful,' Carol said, after he had gone. 'What a grump!'

'Oh, Carol, you're being too hard on him. Maybe he's tired. Or maybe he doesn't like company first thing in the morning.'

'He's worse than my husband,' Carol said, 'and that's saying something. Ted would rather take the dog out for a walk than talk to me in the morning. Men, eh?'

'Men,' Kirsty echoed.

All the same, silly as it seemed, she was a bit disappointed. Bob might have had a little more to say to her. After all, it wasn't as though she was a complete stranger, or someone who chatted on and on about trivia and didn't know when to stop.

★　★　★

After breakfast, Kirsty decided to have a look round those parts of the inn she had not yet seen. Curiosity demanded no less. To her surprise, she discovered rooms she had not suspected.

There was a separate dining room, for example, presumably dating from times when there were more visitors than now.

There were more guest rooms, as well, some of them now no more than huge storage cupboards.

It seemed strange that there was no use for them.

In an area like this, the inn should be booming.

Carol caught up with her.

'Having a good look around?

'You might as well. The weather's not up to much at the moment.'

'Oh, I'll get out in a little while. I was just curious about these unused rooms.

'What a lot of spare capacity the place has.'

Carol nodded. 'Yes. I'd like to have been here in its heyday. It must have been lively and cheerful.

'Here, have you seen this room?' she added.

Carol opened a door Kirsty had not yet reached.

'What do you think?' she said with a flourish.

Kirsty peered into the room. 'Oh, my!'

The centrepiece of the room was a genuine four-poster bed.

'The honeymoon suite,' Carol said.

'You wouldn't believe who's stayed in here over the years.'

'It's lovely,' Kirsty said.

'It's a bit musty,' Carol said. 'I'll open the window.'

She slid the top sash down a few inches and looked out across the lake.

'It's a long time since we had any honeymooners here,' she said, 'but you can see how nice it used to be, can't you?'

'Oh yes,' Kirsty said thoughtfully then added, 'and maybe it will be again.'

'Maybe,' Carol said without conviction.

* * *

Later, Kirsty wandered across the fields around the inn, studying the building from different angles, exploring the thoughts that were beginning to form in her mind.

Since Carol had told her how much the inn was on the market for, her thoughts no longer seemed quite such an impossible pipe dream. Buying the inn was something that might just be financially manageable, if she could ever summon the nerve.

Nobody else seemed to want it. But she did. Very much.

More than ever, in fact.

She would need to sell her mother's house first, and her own little place. Then she would need to sort out a mortgage. Maybe get a commercial mortgage?

That ought to be possible. Why not? And if it was . . . ? Could she do everything that needed doing here? Not at first, perhaps, she knew that. But in time she could.

Then, of course, there was the question of whether she could run an inn.

It was a daunting prospect, something that would be completely new to her, but she couldn't see why not. It wasn't really an inn, or a pub, in the traditional sense. These days it was more a guest house with a licensed restaurant attached. She could do that.

She winced. Was she just being sentimental? Was she in danger of getting in over her head? No. If someone as inept as Harry could run the place for so long, so could she — and a lot better probably. She knew how small businesses worked. She'd seen enough of them.

She would have to make sure Carol stayed, of course. Carol knew the place inside-out. She would promote her. Make her the Deputy Manager or something. Pay her more money, and get her more help.

The chef they had now seemed good, too. She would want to keep him.

Oh, it was so exciting! For the first time in a long time, she had found something she really, really wanted to do.

She had a sense of purpose that she realised had been missing from her life for far too long.

In the late afternoon, Kirsty saw Bob coming down from the hills. She watched him for a few minutes, until he disappeared into a little hidden valley. She smiled and resumed her walk.

Bob, she mused. What a strange man he was.

He was in the bar that evening when she arrived for her meal.

'Good day?' she asked.

'Not bad.'

He looked tired. More than that, he looked dejected, as if he was struggling physically and spiritually. Or ill. He looked ill, she realised.

'Have you eaten yet?'

He shook his head.

She managed not to press him further.

She watched him tip his glass to finish the beer he'd been drinking. 'Is anything wrong?' she asked.

'Wrong?'

'I mean . . . are you all right? You don't look very well. You look . . . tired.'

She only just managed to stop herself saying he looked worn-out.

'Oh, yes. I'm tired, all right.'

'And it's something a good night's sleep can't cure.'

He put his beer glass down, nodded to Kirsty and headed for the door.

She found a seat and ordered a meal, but she no longer felt hungry. She was wondering what was wrong. Bob seemed a different man.

As she was finishing her meal, she noticed a small package on the adjacent table. Something Bob had forgotten or misplaced. She got up and reached for it, and saw then what it was: a box with a prescription label bearing the name, 'Mr Robert Simpson', and a message about how many times a day the contents were to be taken.

She recognised the name of the tablets the box contained and frowned. It was a name that had been familiar in her mother's house after her father had died.

As she looked for Carol to hand the box to, she wondered what on earth a man like Bob was doing with anti-depressants.

A Crushing Disappointment

Kirsty had known Matthew Taylor most of her life. They had been at school together, and he was just about the only person she still knew from those days. She no longer saw much of him, now he had such a rarefied job, but he was the man she had decided to go and see.

'Kirsty Johnson in person!' A big grin spread across Matthew's face. 'How are you, kid?'

'Much better for seeing you, Matthew,' she responded, laughing.

'Ah! Flattery. You must want to borrow some money.'

She grinned happily. He still had a nice, cheeky way with him, even if he was now a bank manager. 'I always knew you would end up in a posh job, Matthew,' she told him.

'I haven't 'ended up' yet. There's a lot more to come. Just you wait and see.'

'I'm pleased for you, Matthew. It's good to see you doing so well.'

'Thanks. So what about you, Kirsty?'

She told him what she was thinking of doing with Fells Inn. He listened thoughtfully. Somehow he managed to acquire cups of coffee for them both without her knowing how he had done it.

'So,' Kirsty concluded, 'I thought I would ask your advice.'

'You really want to do this, don't you?'

'More than anything I've wanted for a long time.'

'And I can see you've looked into it, and thought it through. Well, the bank should be able to help. There's probably no need to sell your house, or your mother's, unless you really want to. I'm sure we'll be able to offer you a commercial mortgage. It's a perfectly viable business you're looking at here. The bank will be eager to support you.

'And so will I,' he added.

Kirsty smiled happily. 'I was really just thinking of a loan to bridge the gap, while I sell the houses,' she said.

'Keep the two things separate, Kirsty, that would be my advice. One isn't dependent on the other. Go ahead and sell if you want to, but you don't have to.'

Matthew made a further proposal. 'If it would help, I would be happy to open negotiations with the vendor's agent on your behalf. See if we can knock the price they're asking down a bit. Do you have their details?'

She liked the idea of 'we'. She liked the thought that she wasn't alone with all this.

★ ★ ★

'Oh, yes,' Joyce said breathlessly. 'Oh yes indeed! What a wonderful idea, Kirsty. Oh, I do hope it comes off for you.'

'I'm glad you approve,' Kirsty said happily. 'It's early days yet, but I had to tell someone.'

'Of course you did. And of course I

approve. Alan does as well, don't you dear?'

'Approve what?' Alan said, looking away from the football match on the television. 'What are you getting me into now, Joyce?'

'Kirsty's going to buy a pub in the Lake District.'

Alan's expression revealed his total astonishment. 'Tell me it's true?' he demanded. 'Tell me she's not making it up?'

'It's an inn, actually,' Kirsty told him happily. 'Not a pub.'

'An inn?'

'Oh, Alan!' Joyce said, 'don't you ever listen?'

'I'm listening now, aren't I?'

Turning back to Kirsty, he said, 'An inn? Will it be the sort of place where old friends can come and stay for their holidays?'

'As often as you like,' she assured him. 'I shall insist on it. And if you do a bit of gardening for me, you'll get free beer as well.'

Alan switched off the television. 'Tell me more.'

She returned to Fells that weekend, eager to have another look at the inn. Soon, she thought, I might not need to make this trip. Soon I might actually be living here.

It was a happy thought, one that made her smile all the way there.

It was only when she reached the bottom of the slope leading into the village that her dreams crashed. She saw in a moment that the 'For Sale' sign outside the inn had been replaced by an 'Under Offer' sign. It was some minutes before she could even bring herself to get out of the car.

Oh, well, she thought with resignation, at least I'll still be able to come here to stay, whoever owns it.

Bob wasn't in any better spirits than she was. He was sitting at one of the outside tables, watching her emerge from the car.

'Hello, Bob.'

'Hi.'

'Been far?'

'Not today.'

He returned to his newspaper. She shrugged and made her way inside. Maybe his pills weren't working, she thought sarcastically. Then she chided herself for being so mean.

She felt flat. It was so disappointing a development that she didn't feel like doing anything at all. Carol wasn't on duty either, which made it worse. Even Henry wasn't around. She had a solitary time of it until Bob reappeared just as she was finishing her evening meal. Having already been rebuffed once by him, she didn't encourage conversation and was surprised when he approached her.

'Tomorrow,' he said.

'Yes, Bob?' she said crisply.

'I'm going up Goat Fell.'

She nodded without much interest. 'Good. Have a nice day.'

'You don't fancy coming along, do you?'

It took a moment for the question to sink in.

'Me?' she said with surprise.

'Well . . . I just wondered.'

She wasn't in the mood. She didn't even feel like talking to him. Then it struck her. This was Bob, remember? The famously solitary, enigmatic Bob. It was a great honour to be asked to go anywere with him. Besides, hadn't she long dreamed of reaching the top of Goat Fell?

'Why not?' she said, trying to make her reply sound as casual as she could. Then, as an afterthought, she added, 'But I'm not an experienced fell walker. You do know that?'

'You'll be fine,' he smiled. 'And I'll be glad of the company. Tomorrow, then?'

'Tomorrow,' she agreed, feeling better. 'An alpine start?'

'Nine sharp.'

A smile spread across her face as he turned and left. What a bundle of surprises the man could be.

A Wonderful Day

Nine sharp, he'd said. She made sure she was standing at the front door with a couple of minutes to spare. 'Nice jacket,' he said, on seeing her waiting for him. 'Is it new?'

'No, no! I've had it a while,' she told him off-handedly, secretly proud he'd noticed.

He glanced at her still shiny boots and her new backpack but didn't say anything else.

'I think I've got everything,' she assured him.

'Including water?'

She nodded. She knew how important it was to take sufficient liquid with you when you were walking in the hills. Dehydration wasn't going to catch her out — not on her first walk with the redoubtable Bob.

'Let's go, then,' he said.

He set off at an agreeably easy pace and she fell in beside him as they headed over the meadows towards the slopes of Goat Fell.

'Will the rain hold off?' she asked.

He glanced up at the white cloud wrapped around the upper slopes of the mountain. 'Maybe.'

'There's confidence for you.'

He chuckled and gave her a warm smile that augured well for the day.

Bob was considerate. When they started climbing, he set a pace that was comfortable for Kirsty and he paused frequently to allow her to catch her breath. Her confidence grew. She could cope, she decided. She could keep up.

'You're doing well,' he told her at one point.

'Better than I expected,' she admitted with a smile.

He laughed. She was pleased. Making him laugh felt good.

They made steady progress. It was

warm without being too hot. And Kirsty found the going easier than the last time she had been on her own on the mountain. Something to do with having a companion, she supposed.

They reached the tarn in an hour and spent a little time there, lingering over a cup of coffee from the flask Bob produced from his rucksack.

'Beautiful, isn't it?' Kirsty murmured.

Bob nodded. 'And peaceful,' he added. 'So peaceful.'

She wondered if that was what it was about for him. Peacefulness. It seemed important to him. She sensed how relaxed he was now, as if the tranquillity of this place and the effort to get here had dissolved whatever it was that normally stressed him.

'Unexplored territory for me, from now on,' Kirsty said, glancing upwards towards the still hidden summit.

'Lucky you. All that to come,' Bob said. 'Come on.'

It was harder after that. The path was

much steeper above the tarn, and soon they had left the heather and grass behind and entered a world of bare jagged rock and scree.

Kirsty was excited, even more so when the way ahead began to fade in and out of view as the cloud shifted and swirled around them.

She had never been anywhere like this before. Yet she was not apprehensive. On the contrary, she was thrilled, exhilarated. She felt she was beginning to sense some of what climbers must feel, the powerful attraction that draws them back to the mountains time after time.

Goat Fell wasn't Everest, but for her it was close enough.

Another hour, nearer two, then suddenly they were there. Impressively, the cloud cleared, as if on cue, to reveal a broad stony expanse, the summit plateau. They made for the rough cairn at the centre, where generations of climbers had built what had begun as a simple pile of stones into a large monument. Kirsty added a stone of her own. Then they settled down to lunch.

'This is wonderful, Bob. To be here . . . Thank you so much for inviting me along. All these months I've been wondering what it was like up here.'

'And I wondered what it was that kept bringing you back to Fells. So it was sheer curiosity?'

'Envy, more like. I wanted to do what you were doing but I didn't have the nerve on my own.'

He laughed. 'You can't beat it,' he said. 'Up here, on top of the world. There's nothing finer.'

They were in agreement about that, she thought happily.

★ ★ ★

For a while they sat in silent contentment, gazing at the panoramic view below them.

Then Kirsty's thoughts turned to other matters. She wondered whether to tell Bob what had been on her mind when she arrived in Fells. She wasn't sure, but this seemed a good time to broach the subject.

'Today has made up for the disappointment I experienced when I arrived yesterday,' she began.

He glanced curiously at her.

'The 'Under Offer' sign at the inn,' she added, by way of explanation.

'Oh, that.'

'Yes, that. I'd become so used to seeing the 'For Sale' sign. You see, I'd been making plans to make my own offer for the inn.

'So I was very disappointed to see someone had beaten me to it.'

'Really?' he said, turning to stare at her.

'Really.' She nodded and went on to tell him of her hopes, and how they had been dashed.

'You must really like the old place?'

'Oh, I do. I'd been in love with the memory of it since I was a little girl, and now I've rediscovered it.

'Besides, I need a new direction in

my life. I've been drifting along for such a long time now, going nowhere, doing nothing. And I'm sick of it.

'I was getting to the point where I no longer liked myself. The idea of taking over the inn, the challenge of it, changed all that.'

She shrugged. 'Now I'll have to find something else.'

'Well,' Bob said, 'it's not over yet.'

'There's no fat lady singing here, Bob. Of course it's over.

'Someone has come in ahead of me. After all this time, as well.'

'It's only under offer. The deal isn't done yet. The offer might fall through.

'Anyway,' Bob went on, 'even if everything does go ahead, the old place won't change much. It will still be at the foot of Goat Fell, whatever happens.'

'I guess.' She shrugged and gave him a wan smile. 'It won't be the same, though, will it? Not for me.'

'Perhaps not.'

The air began to stir around them.

Kirsty glanced round and saw Bob looking at fresh cloud on a neighbouring peak.

'Come on,' he said, beginning to stuff things back into his rucksack. 'A change is on the way. Time for us to get moving.'

They made good time on the way down, managing to keep ahead of the rain. All that effort to get up here, Kirsty thought with a wry smile, and now we're racing to get down.

Bob gave her some useful insights on the way down, like how to half-turn and slide on loose scree, and how to move quickly, with confidence, and not worry about the possibility of falling.

'If you worry about it, you will fall,' he told her. 'Just get on with it. And if you do fall, relax and pick yourself up again. It won't be the end of the world.'

'It's all right you saying that,' Kirsty said with a laugh. 'You're not the one who's likely to fall, are you?'

'I've done plenty of it,' he assured her. 'It's nothing to be scared about.

You'll likely just get mucky hands and knees.'

She laughed again. She couldn't help thinking it wasn't the sort of advice she would ever have got from Craig.

'It's like driving,' Bob said. 'When you go out in your car, you don't worry all the time that you might crash, do you? If you did, you wouldn't be able to drive at all. You'd never get started.'

'And in the mountains you don't worry you might fall. You'd never leave the valley if you did. It's the same thing.'

Kirsty wasn't convinced, but she could see what he was trying to say. So she got on with it, as he suggested. If she fell, she decided, she would just have to deal with it when it happened.

And that was what she did. Because she did fall, of course. Once or twice she slipped on loose stones. But it was no big deal, she discovered. She just picked herself up and got on with it. Exactly as Bob was doing, she realised with a wry smile, as she saw him dusting himself off after a slip.

So he wasn't infallible.

Trying to move with more confidence didn't prevent leg muscles she hadn't known she possessed complaining, though, and by the time they reached the valley floor she felt like a seasoned mountaineer. Weary, aching, muddy — and satisfied and happy.

'It's a hot shower for me now,' she announced as they approached Fells Inn. 'But in a couple of hours I'm sure I'll be hungry. Perhaps we could meet up for a meal together?'

Bob seemed to spend a few moments thinking it over. Then he nodded. 'Sounds good to me,' he agreed. 'Seven be OK with you?'

She smiled through her fatigue and promised herself a glass of white wine to celebrate her achievements today: reaching the summit of Goat Fell and making Bob laugh.

Quite a day.

A Surprising Evening

Bob was in a different mood that evening. Kirsty sensed it immediately. He was pleasant, open, more at ease. Something had changed, possibly for the better.

He stood up as she approached the table and pulled out a chair for her.

'Thank you.' She sat down and then slumped in an exaggerated fashion. 'Are you as weary as me, Bob, after today?'

'You get used to it,' he said with a chuckle. 'I've been up there more times than I've had hot dinners.'

'How often do you come here, then?'

He looked at her and shrugged. 'Quite often, I suppose. No pattern, though. Just when I feel like it. I'm self-employed, so I can please myself.'

She left it there. But she realised now

what the difference was. He was talking more easily about himself. Perhaps because he was more used to her. But she felt it would still be best to take it easy, and avoid seeming to interrogate him on his life.

Carol appeared with their meals. If she thought it surprising they were sitting together, she gave no hint of it.

'Cumbrian sausage,' she said, placing Bob's plate before him, 'and chicken curry for you, Madam.'

'Is it very spicy?' Kirsty asked.

'It might be,' Carol advised cautiously. 'Chef isn't in a good mood.'

But it was fine. Very nice. Just right after a day in the hills.

'The food here is always pretty good,' Kirsty commented to Bob.

'Oh, I like everything here,' he said, and added, 'there's nowhere I'd rather be.'

'You like the peace and the quiet?'

'It's just about the only place I do feel at peace.' It was a strange remark. Kirsty didn't know what to make of it.

108

They ate in silence for a little while. Then she ventured, 'Is Fells better than home?'

He gave her a wry smile. 'I don't really have a home any more. I used to. Now I just have a house, an empty house.'

Oh, dear. She waited for him to tell her in his own way — if he wanted to tell her at all. 'Three years ago,' Bob said slowly, 'my family was destroyed in a single day. I lost my wife and two sons.'

Kirsty pushed her plate aside. 'Bob,' she said gently, 'don't say anything you don't want to. You don't have to explain anything to me.'

'It's all right. It's no secret.'

'We'd rented a villa in Greece for a couple of weeks. The first holiday in a long time. Beautiful place. The kids loved it. We all did.'

'One night my wife persuaded me to go by myself to a local bar where we knew they would have a Man U football game on the telly. She knew I would

109

like to see it, but she and the kids couldn't sit in a bar all evening. Anyway, she said they needed an early night.'

'So I went, had a couple of beers, watched the game, wandered back happy as a king. I thought they were all asleep. It was a long time before I realised they weren't.'

Kirsty's heart was pounding. She felt sick with dread. She stared and waited, not sure she wanted to hear any more but unable not to listen.

'Faulty water heater, they said at the enquiry. Carbon monoxide poisoning. None of them even woke up.'

'I'm so sorry, Bob.' There were tears in her eyes as she gripped his hand. 'I had no idea.'

He just shrugged.

She knew now what his prescription was for. If anyone had a right to be depressed, it was him.

'What about you?' Bob asked. 'What about your life?'

'Me? Nothing much to say, really. I

110

live alone. Boring job. My long-time boyfriend and I called it a day recently. My mum died a couple of years ago. No other family that I'm in contact with.'

'So you come here?'

She nodded. 'I needed something new in my life, and it seemed like fate when the inn appeared.

'I used to come here as a child with Mum and Dad, and I always remembered it as a place where I was happy. So I came back to see what it was like now, and I fell in love with it all over again. Then I got to thinking about relieving poor Henry of his burden and taking it on myself. I realised I could put it to rights, and enjoy myself doing it. Make a new life for myself, as well. Anyway,' she concluded with a shrug, 'it's over now, that dream.'

'Not necessarily,' Bob said slowly. 'I think the offer has been withdrawn.'

She looked sharply at him.

'The board is down, I noticed. Go and see for yourself.'

She did, and saw it was true. The 'Under Offer' sign had reverted to a 'For Sale' sign.

* * *

'Those signs go up and down like yo-yo's,' Bob said. 'Estate agents, eh?'

Kirsty turned and saw that he had followed her outside.

'It's wonderful,' she said with delight, hardly daring to believe it.

She reached out to hug him and plant a kiss on his cheek. He hugged her back, laughing. She laughed with him and looked up. Then, surprising her, he kissed her. He kissed her properly. She closed her eyes and responded.

'Sorry, Kirsty,' he said, pulling away.

'Don't be,' she said softly.

Only later did she realise fully what had happened, and wondered what had come over them both.

Nothing, she decided. Nothing — and yet everything.

A Shock Is In Store

The next morning, disappointingly but perhaps predictably, Bob was already gone when Kirsty appeared for breakfast.

'Disappeared into the gloom,' Carol said, gazing out of the window. 'Probably exhausted from all the talking he did last night,' she added, giving Kirsty a pointed look.

'Carol! Don't be so mean. We had our evening meal together. That was all.'

'If you say so.' Carol wore a severe look for a moment longer. Then she chuckled and smiled. 'Actually, I was pleased to see the two of you sitting together. It was good for you both to have a bit of company for a change.'

Kirsty laughed happily. 'What would

I do without you, Carol? You remind me of my mother.'

Carol scowled and went back to the kitchen.

★ ★ ★

All the way home, and long after she got there, there were just two things on Kirsty's mind. One was Bob, and the confused feelings she had for him. His kiss lingered on her lips, as did the insight she had been given into his life and circumstances.

Poor man. Losing his family like that. He had a big load to carry. No wonder he needed time and space to himself. No wonder he was sometimes depressed.

Yet he was good company when he let his guard down, and she'd really enjoyed their day together. She'd enjoyed their brief moment of intimacy, too.

What on earth had come over them both? All in all, it was an experience, brief though it had been, that convinced her she had been right to split up with Craig. It was a long time since she had felt so thrilled to be in a man's arms.

What a pity Bob had gone the next morning. She wondered why he had. They'd parted on good terms. Nothing had been said the night before, but it had been understood, certainly by her, that it was the start of something, not the end.

He must have had his work to go to, she decided. Whatever that was.

She had to be practical. He stole time away from his work, but he would have commitments he couldn't avoid. She shouldn't read too much into his departure. It didn't mean he regretted what had happened. Not at all.

She would see him next time she went to Fells. No need to wonder and agonise. She would see him again. Of that, she was certain.

★ ★ ★

The other matter on Kirsty's mind was the very practical question of whether or not to resurrect her bid for the inn. Had the other offer really been withdrawn?

It was worth enquiring. You never knew.

The question became increasingly pressing as her first day back at work wore on. In the end, she decided there was only one way to find out for sure. There was no point speculating. She really had better ask.

The next morning, she rang Fells Inn. To her surprise, Henry answered. Cautiously, she explained her interest and asked what the situation was. Had the previous offer really been withdrawn?

Henry sounded even more weary and dispirited than usual. 'Who knows?' he said. 'Bob changes his mind from one day to the next.'

'Bob?'

'Bob Simpson. That guy who's always here. You must have seen him?'

116

'Yes. I know who Bob is. But what's he got to do with it?'

'It was his offer that got withdrawn, wasn't it?'

Kirsty was shocked. For a moment she didn't know what to say. Had she misheard? Was Henry joking?

'Are you serious?' she asked finally.

'Of course I am. And I'm sick to death of him, as well as this dump. So make me an offer — please!'

She was so stunned by the surprise news that she took an early lunch break. She sat in a corner of her favourite café and pondered. But she didn't really know what to think, or to do. That was the truth of it. She was in a state of total confusion. Panic, almost.

So it really was Bob that had made the offer? She had to accept that it was. But why on earth hadn't he said anything to her? He'd had plenty of opportunity when they were talking things over. And when I was foolishly revealing my hopes and dreams, she thought bitterly. Not to mention being held in his arms, and beginning to dream. Oh, what a fool I was! What on earth must he have thought of me?

Well, she might have been stupid, but Bob had been pretty sneaky, not saying anything. She was surprised at that. Shocked even. And disappointed. She'd thought she was getting to know him. She'd thought he was a kind and decent man, and had even begun to harbour faint hopes that their friendship might grow into something more. Wrong — again!

Her mood changed. Bewilderment gave way to anger. What on earth was he playing at? Why hadn't he told her of his interest in the inn?

She could find no answer to those questions. None at all. Just to contemplate them made her feel unutterably depressed. They also took away all her enthusiasm for the inn. She just couldn't contemplate it any more.

So she would forget about it all and get on with her life.

It wasn't as if she had nothing to do.

Going to work and being responsible for two houses was more than enough, she told herself. She didn't need a man and a dilapidated old inn, as well.

* * *

Joyce wasn't so sure. 'It's no good stopping in a job you don't like,' she said. 'Life's too short for that.'

'I do like it. Whatever gave you the idea I didn't?'

'You did,' Joyce said, laughing.

'Well . . . ' Kirsty smiled reluctantly and conceded the point. 'But I don't really dislike it,' she went on. 'My job is very interesting. Dealing with furniture from all over the world. Sorting out problems. Working with people I like. It's just that . . . '

'You're fed up with it. You fancy a change — or you did.'

Kirsty nodded. 'How well you know me, Joyce.'

'I ought to, by now.'

'But I've got past that point now.

119

That was just me feeling a bit unsettled.'

'Yes?' Joyce said dubiously.

'I'm happy again now.'

Joyce just looked at her.

'Really. I am.'

'Well, you should know.'

It was true, Kirsty reflected. She should. But she didn't. She was determined to put recent happenings behind her, and was hoping she could, but . . . Joyce was right. She had wanted a change.

Oh, it was all so difficult!

The inn would have been too big a challenge for her, anyway. She wouldn't have been able to cope with it all, especially on her own. It was time she stopped dreaming and sorted herself out. Lived the life she had, instead of trying to create a new one that in all probability would have been a disaster.

'You haven't told me yet,' Joyce said.

'Told you what?'

'Why the change of mind, or heart.'

'Well, one problem is I've got too

much to do. Work, two houses . . . '

'Sell one,' Joyce said crisply. 'You're never going to live in your mother's house, are you? So sell it. You can't leave it standing empty. Get it on the market. Right now.'

'Is it the right time of year?'

'Never mind that. Get it valued and on the market. Do it today!'

Kirsty wasn't sure. She had intended selling, of course, but now her enthusiasm for Fells Inn had waned, the urgency was gone. She didn't need to sell it. She could wait.

'Just do it, Kirsty,' Joyce insisted, breaking into her thoughts.

Kirsty nodded and smiled. 'You're right, I suppose. There's no point dithering any longer, is there?'

'None at all.'

They sat in silence for a moment. 'You still haven't told me why you changed your mind,' Joyce said.

'About what? Fells Inn?'

Joyce nodded.

Kirsty looked at her friend and

grimaced. I have to tell someone sometime, I suppose, she thought with a sigh. Why not Joyce?

'There's this man,' she began.

'I knew it!'

'Have I told you about Bob? Well, actually, there's not that much to tell,' Kirsty said, already feeling slightly ridiculous. 'I mean, nothing much happened between us.

'It's just that . . .'

'Something must have happened, Kirsty.'

It was easier once she got started. And it didn't sound so ridiculous, either.

When she had finished, Joyce wasn't judgmental.

If anything, she was very supportive.

'Maybe you should separate the man from the inn?' she suggested. 'Be practical. Forget about Bob. You were interested in the inn before you got to know him, weren't you? So nothing has changed really.'

Kirsty sighed. 'You're right in one

way,' she admitted, 'but something has changed. How I feel about it has changed.'

'All because of Bob?'

'Silly, isn't it?'

'I wouldn't say that. But maybe second thoughts are a good idea. Maybe you're seeing problems now you didn't see before.'

Kirsty nodded.

'Take your time,' Joyce suggested. 'Don't give up on it. But don't rush into something you're not sure about, either.

'Think it through a bit more.'

'I'm a little afraid it might be too big a challenge for me,' Kirsty admitted.

'It will be a challenge. Of course it will. But you've got it in you to meet it, Kirsty.

'I know you. If you want to do something badly enough, you can do it. I know you can.'

It was nice to hear such reassurance, Kirsty thought.

But was Joyce right? Did she really

have it in her to deal with everything
that would be involved?

She wasn't sure any more.

She had thought she was. But now
she just didn't know.

She felt so flat.

'You really like him, don't you?' Joyce
said softly.

Kirsty nodded.

'I can tell,' Joyce said with a smile.
'Well, maybe he'll get in touch.'

'Maybe.'

* * *

Kirsty supposed it would be good if
Bob did get in touch. But it seemed
unlikely. In any case, he had deceived
her.

How could she ever accept that? He
should have said something.

'He should have told me he had put
in an offer for the inn,' she said heatedly
to Joyce. 'Really he should.'

'I agree,' Joyce said, 'he should. But
he's a man, isn't he?'

'And we all know what men are like, don't we?'

'Yes,' Kirsty said, nodding. It was the old refrain. 'We do.'

'Well, if we've got that one settled,' Joyce said, 'how about doing some Christmas shopping in the Metrocentre?'

'It's August, Joyce.'

'You can never start too soon. Besides, we'll miss the crowds if we start now.'

'And they won't have run out of anything yet, I know!' Kirsty began to laugh. 'Oh, Joyce, you know how to cheer me up. Come on, then. Let's go.'

Kirsty Is In Turmoil

Joyce was right. Being decisive did help. It helped a lot. Instead of feeling at the mercy of ocean currents and winds she couldn't influence, Kirsty began to feel more in control of her life.. She stopped dithering. She took decisions. Even if she didn't know where she was going in the long run, there were still things she could do right now.

The first thing she did was exactly what Joyce had urged her to do. She put her mother's house up for sale. The agent who valued it surprised her, suggesting a figure far higher than she'd expected.

'Are you sure?' she said dubiously.

'Oh, yes. We've had a couple go around here in recent weeks for much the same price. It's a nice area, and people know it as such. You won't have any difficulty selling this one.'

'It seems a lot of money.'

'That's an unusual point of view,' the agent said. 'Most people think they'll be robbed if they sell at the price we value the house at.'

Kirsty trusted Mr Edgar, the estate agent.

'People, eh?' she said, smiling. 'What do they know? Well, you must know what it's worth. I'm very lucky.'

'It's a nice house in a good location,' Mr Edgar re-affirmed. 'It wants a bit doing to it, of course. Nothing serious. Updating, mostly. Decorating. New windows, maybe. New kitchen. Possibly a new bathroom, as well. That sort of thing.'

Kirsty nodded. She had expected that. The house her mum had been happy with for forty years wasn't one many twenty-something, newly-wed young couples would want today.

'But that's nothing out of the ordinary,' Mr Edgar concluded. 'You can pretty well say the same thing about any house that comes on the market these days. A lot of the so-called improvements are unnecessary, in my opinion, but most people feel they have to make them.'

'Really?'

He nodded. 'I blame these make-over programmes on television. All the young ones want this month's fashion. Then, in a year's time, they want what was there originally. So they go hunting round architectural scrap yards looking fruitlessly for the marble fireplaces they threw out when they first bought the house. So then they buy new Victorian fireplaces — made in China last week.'

He paused, shrugged and added, 'We're fast losing our traditions.'

'You'll be more aware of that than most of us,' Kirsty said, trying to be agreeable, but wondering secretly if there was anything at all worth salvaging in her mother's house. Now she'd collected her moth-eaten teddy bear, with its one remaining ear, she couldn't think of one single thing. And she didn't think even Mr Edgar would count Teddy as an architectural treasure.

Mr Edgar hadn't finished. 'The important thing to remember, is that whatever you do to a house, you can't change the location. And basically location determines price. So this house will sell quickly at the price I've suggested. If you're happy with it, that is?' he added, eyebrows raised in enquiry.

'Oh, yes,' Kirsty assured him

★ ★ ★

'What did he say?' Joyce asked Kirsty.

'Who?'

'The estate agent. Who else?'

'It was very satisfactory. Mum's house is worth more than I realised. And he thinks it will sell quickly.'

'That's good.' Joyce looked pleased. 'I'm happy you took my advice, in that case.'

'Oh, Joyce, I always listen to what you say.

'You're such an intelligent, know-ledgeable, authoritative, impressive sort of person.'

'Hang on a minute. I want to write all that down to show Alan. I'm obviously seriously under-appreciated at home.'

'I'll tell him, Joyce. Next time I see him I'll let him know what a jewel he's got.'

'Good.'

'So that's one thing settled. Your mother's house, I mean,' she added.

'Yes,' Kirsty said. 'It's a relief to get the ball rolling on that.'

'Don't give up, Kirsty. Don't ever give up.'

'What do you mean?'

'Like I said, don't give up on the things that are important to you.'

She paused and then added, 'We didn't.'

'Who didn't?'

'Me and Alan. Alan and I, rather.'

Kirsty stared at her for a moment. 'Oh, Joyce! You aren't pregnant?'

Joyce smiled and nodded.

'Oh, Joyce, that's wonderful! Oh, congratulations. I'm so happy for you both.'

'Thank you, Kirsty. So don't you give up either. Promise?'

'Never,' she assured her friend.

★ ★ ★

Kirsty still didn't know what to do about Fells Inn. Whenever she thought about it, she would become upset about the way Bob had misled her. Somehow that had taken the shine off her enthusiasm. So she waited to see if it would recover.

She was even more ambivalent about Bob himself. On the one hand, she had come to like him so much, and she hadn't forgotten the thrill of 'that kiss', as she thought of it. On the other hand, how could you trust a man who would lie to your face?

Well, not lie as such, perhaps, but mislead you. Not tell you things that were obviously important. Listen to you describing your hopes and dreams, and not tell you he was in a position to stop you achieving them. It didn't bear thinking about. You could never trust a man like that.

Craig wasn't a bit like that, Kirsty thought. He might be dull and boring, and complacent and self-satisfied, and a few other things as well, but he would never carry on like that. If he had an interest in a property, he would make sure the whole world knew about it. It would become part of the Craig success story.

She smiled ruefully and shook her head. She had better not go down that road again. Craig was her past, not her future. But, then, so was Bob. She wasn't going down that road, either.

Unfortunately, that seemed to mean forgetting about Fells Inn, as well. She couldn't think of having one without the other. That was just the way it was.

The way she was.

Joyce didn't understand, of course. Joyce was so relentlessly practical it wasn't true.

'Business is business,' she said crisply. 'A man is something else. Keep them separate.'

It was all right for her to say something like that, Kirsty thought.

That was what being married to Alan all those years had done for her. Joyce had no idea.

'How can you say that, Joyce?' she said with irritation. 'That is the most ridiculous thing I have ever heard. After all I've told you, as well.'

'I'm just being practical, Kirsty,' Joyce said with a shrug. Then she smiled. 'You're very fond of this Bob, aren't you?'

'Well, maybe I was. Briefly.'

'More than that, I think.'

'For goodness' sake, Joyce! I've forgotten about him already.'

'I can see that.'

After a pause, Joyce smiled and said,

'Don't mind me, Kirsty. I'm only teasing. What I would do, if I were in your shoes . . . '

'Which you haven't been for many years.'

'Admittedly. Not for quite a while. But I haven't forgotten what it's like when you meet someone you really like, whatever you may think.'

Kirsty relented. 'Oh, Joyce. I'm sorry. I know you mean well. It's just that . . . I've been so miserable. I mean, here I am, getting on with practical things, like you said I should, and I'm just plain miserable. More than ever.'

'I know you are. So what I would do is contact Bob and have it out with him. Talk to him. Maybe there's some simple explanation for what happened, or didn't happen.'

Kirsty shook her head. 'I don't think so, Joyce. I really don't think so.'

Kirsty Makes A Change

What was she to make of Bob's astonishing deception? Kirsty went round and round with it. Her head was buzzing. During the day she could think of little else. At night she couldn't sleep. Everything had been so promising.

She had been so happy. Now this. 'Are you all right, Kirsty?' Emma, her friend at the office, asked.

'Me? Of course.'

'Only you don't seem quite right. I wondered if you were coming down with something. All the rest of us have had the bug. Maybe it's your turn.'

'Maybe it is.' Kirsty did her best to smile reassuringly. 'I'm all right, Emma, thanks. Just tired.'

Emma nodded. 'If you want a hand?'

she added, gesturing towards Kirsty's unusually piled-high in-tray.

'Thanks. I'll give you a shout if I do.'

Emma retreated. At least, Kirsty thought, she's pulled me out of my nosedive to nowhere. The last few days I've let things slip.

She grabbed the item on top of her in-tray and attacked it with vigour. She was re-energised, and she stayed that way for the rest of the day.

By the time she got home that evening, she had sorted out her priorities and intentions. She would, she had decided, go ahead after all. She would ignore the distraction of Bob and seek to buy Fells Inn. Whatever Bob was up to, it had nothing to do with her.

She was disappointed in him, of course she was. But Joyce was right. Her interest in the inn pre-dated her interest in Bob.

The next morning, she phoned her friendly bank manager, Matthew Taylor, and told him she wished to go ahead with the transaction. He was pleased for her, and undertook to prepare both the application for a commercial mortgage and to conduct negotiations with Henry's agent over the sale of the inn.

'Be bold, Kirsty,' he advised, not sounding like a bank manager at all, 'and live life to the full. Never be afraid of a challenge. You're going to have an exciting time.'

'I hope so,' she said. 'I really do.'

* * *

Next, she contacted Mr Edgar, the estate agent, and told him she wished to put her own house on the market as well as her mother's.

'It's a good time to do it,' he said, 'if that's what you're thinking of doing. Despite the doom and gloom merchants down south, not to mention the BBC, the market is very good up here. We've had a few enquiries about your mother's house already, and I'm pretty sure the last couple I took round are going to come back with an offer.'

'Really? That's quick.'

'And my advice to you would be to consider the offer carefully when it comes, but don't feel you have to grab the first one you get. This is an attractive property, and you shouldn't settle for less than my valuation.'

'That's wonderful, Mr Edgar. Thank you so much.'

After that they arranged a time for him to come to value her own house.

Then, greatly cheered, she rang Joyce.

'Told you!' Joyce said. 'Told you so.'

'You're not supposed to say things like that, Joyce.' Kirsty chuckled. 'You're supposed to say, be careful, are you sure, do you think it's the right thing to do? A good friend is supposed to introduce a note of caution, to stop me doing something that I might regret later.'

'Not this one,' Joyce said firmly. 'I say, get on with it, girl.'

Matthew told her Henry's agent had accepted her offer.

'That's great! Thank you so much, Matthew. Was it difficult?'

'Not really, no. They grabbed my hand off. I think the property has been on the market a long time. They were desperate to sell. We could probably have beaten them down a bit further.'

'I wouldn't have wanted that. I want to pay a fair price for the inn.'

'Well, I think you have. So it's over to you, Miss Sunshine. It's all yours. How do you feel?'

She laughed. 'Numb. That's how I feel.'

'It'll wear off. Then you'll feel totally exhilarated. If you don't, let me know. Something will be wrong, and I'll have to try to wriggle you out of it.'

'Don't even think that, Matthew. I'm very happy. It's wonderful. And thank you again so much. You can have the best room in the place for free.'

'Kirsty! Kirsty! That's no way to run a business. I can see you have a lot to learn. When you open up, you'll find friends you didn't even know you had coming to visit you. Charge them top price.'

'What a cynic you've become, Matthew Taylor. I'll do no such thing.'

'I know you won't, Kirsty. You're far too good a human being for that. You'd never make a bank manager. On the other hand, I think you'll do very well indeed running Fells Inn. Good luck, Kirsty — and take care.'

She smiled. Right. That was done. So the next thing to do was visit Fells and talk business.

★ ★ ★

Henry was different. He didn't seem at all like the man she had met on her first visit to Fells Inn.

'Of course,' he said solemnly, 'it will be a big wrench to leave the old place. I still don't know if I'm doing the right thing.'

'I understand,' Kirsty said, equally solemnly.

'My whole life has been spent here.'

'So far,' she pointed out.

He nodded. 'So far.'

She wondered if that was a tear in the corner of his eye.

'So many beautiful mornings,' he droned on. 'Wonderful friends, too. Customers who are the salt of the earth. And the view of the lake and the mountains.

'I shall miss it. Oh, how I shall miss it all!'

'Henry?'

'Mm?'

'What a fraud you are. You won't be able to get out fast enough. You must think I was born yesterday.'

'Kirsty! How can you say such a thing?' he said, looking quite devastated.

'Because I've come to know you so well, Henry. So where will you go now?'

'Blackpool,' he said crisply. 'I've got

my heart set on a little place on the Golden Mile.'

'Bright lights and people?'

'Exactly. Kirsty, can I tell you something in confidence?'

She nodded.

'You're welcome to this old dump.'

* * *

Henry was fair when it came to sorting out transfer arrangements and the price he wanted for various items that were not part of the sale.

'They're mostly worn out, anyway,' he said, speaking of the furniture and fittings. 'If you can use it, keep it. Otherwise . . . ' He stopped and looked thoughtfully at Kirsty. 'I hope it suits you here, Kirsty. I hope things work out well for you. I really do. And I'll let you into a secret.'

'What?'

'In a way, I will be sorry to leave. Truly. Don't tell anyone, but I'll miss the old place. Look after it for me.

Make it a success!'

'I'll do my best, Henry. I really will. Thank you.'

'Now I must go and have a word with Carol.

'You should keep her on. She's worth her weight in gold.'

'Oh, I know. Don't worry, there's no way I could let Carol go.'

'That's it, then,' Henry said, looking relieved, as if the last problem weighing on his mind had been resolved.

'And good luck to you, too, Henry,' Kirsty said. 'I wish you all the best. You're a far nicer man than you like people to think.'

'I'm just in the wrong place,' he said with a grin.

★ ★ ★

Carol was thrilled to hear that Kirsty was to take over the inn.

'That's absolutely fabulous. Oh, what good news. I can't think of anything I'd rather hear.'

Kirsty smiled. 'Thank you, Carol. I'm pleased you feel that way.'

'Oh, I do!'

'Then perhaps you'll stay?'

'What do you mean?'

'Well, new ownership. You might not fancy the idea. You might be thinking of following Henry to Blackpool.'

Carol laughed. 'I didn't know. Is that where he's going?'

'Apparently.'

'That makes a difference. I wonder what my old man and the kids would think if I went off to Blackpool?

'They probably wouldn't miss me, would they?'

Kirsty grinned. 'Not as much as I would, if you left here. What do I need to offer to get you to stay?'

'A kind word now and again? Wages paid on time? Help? An end to moaning and complaining every day?'

'Done! Carol, I want you to be the Assistant Manager. In effect, I want the two of us to run the place. You know how it works, I don't. I'm new here. So we'll do it together. And I'll make sure your wage reflects your true value to Fells Inn. How does that sound? Interested?'

'Sounds good.' Carol smiled with delight. 'We'll get the old place going between us.'

'Good. By the way, thinking about the help you'll need, do you know anyone we might offer a job to?'

'Oh, yes. There are one or two girls I'd like to bring in. Workers, you know.' She grimaced and added, 'Henry only ever wanted to take on the pretty ones. He was never very interested in the girls who just wanted to do a good day's work.'

'I realised that soon after I started coming here,' Kirsty said with a smile.

'I'll start having a word with one or two girls I know,' Carol said. 'I'll get them to come in to see you.'

'Right. That's probably as far as we can go just now. We'll talk again a bit nearer the hand-over date.'

Kirsty sighed. 'My goodness. There's

a lot to sort out.

'You'll have to help me, Carol.'

'Don't worry about that. Who do you think has been running the place the last few years? Henry?'

'Now, now! Henry has been very nice to me today.'

'I'm sure he has.'

'He must think he's won the lottery, finding a buyer for this place. He'll probably move to Blackpool this afternoon!'

It was working out, Kirsty thought. Working out nicely.

Everyone happy and satisfied.

'There's just one thing, Kirsty?'

'What's that?'

'I'm sorry it hasn't worked out for you and Bob. I had hoped you two would get together. I'm sorry.'

Kirsty shrugged. 'That's life, Carol. We can't have everything, can we?'

Right at that moment, she almost convinced herself of that. Bob was water under the bridge. Almost.

A New Life

There was so much to see to as hand-over day approached. There were suppliers to be contacted. Banking arrangements to be made. Utility companies to be approached. A drinks licence to be applied for. Launderers to be contacted.

There were staff to be recruited. An accountant to be consulted. The businessplan to be fine-tuned and put into effect. It was almost too much. Always Kirsty felt as if she were balanced on the edge of a giant wave that might or might not bring her safely ashore.

Kirsty couldn't have managed without Carol. She couldn't have coped at all.

'You know so much about the place, Carol,' she said.

'I ought to. I've grown up here. I've been here since Henry's parents had it. There's not much about this old place that I haven't had to mend or sort out over the years.'

Kirsty smiled. 'I couldn't have done it without you. I would never have got this far.'

'Nonsense. You'd have managed. Anyway, we're nearly there now.'

'Nearly.'

Kirsty frowned. The man from the bank was coming to talk to her tomorrow about the report from the second survey of the building.

She'd wanted him just to tell her on the phone, so she could get on with everything, but he hadn't wanted to do that. It was something he needed to do face-to-face, he'd said.

Meanwhile, the sale of her mother's house was proceeding nicely, and Mr Edgar had high hopes that the sale of her own house wouldn't be far behind.

★ ★ ★

148

With some reluctance, and even more trepidation, Kirsty had given her job up a week or two ago.

'We're all coming to see you, you know,' Emma promised. 'Let us know as soon as you get settled.'

'Yeah,' young Jason echoed, 'we're coming. We're going to hire one of them things, what do you call them? Them things they used to have before they got buses?'

'Charabancs?' Kirsty asked whimsically.

'That'll do. I was thinking trams, but a chary-what's-it will do. Better get a decent beer in, as well. We won't want any of that Cumbrian rubbish.'

'It's going to be a temperance guest house,' Kirsty joked.

'Temperance? Never heard of it. Where's that beer from?'

'Get on with you!' Emma said. 'But we will come,' she assured Kirsty again. 'Just as soon as you give us the word.'

'Keep my job warm,' Kirsty said with a wry smile, 'in case it doesn't work out.'

'Oh, it will!' they chorused.

With that, she left the office, daring to hope her friends would be proved right.

★ ★ ★

Now Joyce was coming for her first look round. Alan, too. Kirsty was on tenterhooks. She was so excited. She couldn't wait to show them around. In fact, she couldn't wait to see if they could even find Fells.

But they did.

'This where you are!' Alan called, as their car drew to a halt. 'We've been all over the Lake District!'

'Do you mean to tell me, Alan, that Joyce can't read a map?' Kirsty called.

'It wasn't that. I just didn't believe him,' Joyce said, rushing to greet her.

Kirsty gave her a hug.

Alan gave Kirsty a peck on the cheek. 'My, oh my!' he said, 'just look at it. What a place!'

All three gazed at Fells Inn.

'It looks lovely,' Joyce said excitedly. 'Can we go inside?'

'That's why you've come, isn't it? Of course you can.'

'Quite a place,' Alan murmured. 'I'm impressed already. And all yours, eh, Kirsty?'

'Not yet. Not quite. This is a sort of transitional period. I'm working myself in before the contracts are exchanged.'

★   ★   ★

They went inside. Kirsty showed them around. A couple of customers offered cheerful greetings.

Carol arrived. 'Hello, both of you. Welcome! Kirsty told me you were coming. Tea, anyone? Drinks? Food? Lunch?'

Kirsty laughed and they settled for lunch.

Kirsty and Joyce shared a pot of tea. Alan decided he needed to sample the local ale. It was a nice beginning. The day was unfolding as well as Kirsty could have hoped.

Later, when lunch was over, Alan got into a conversation with the chef about football and Kirsty and Joyce were left alone.

'It's lovely, Kirsty. Wonderful. I can see why you fell in love with the place,' Joyce said.

'You really do like it, Joyce? You don't think I'm making a mistake?'

'Of course not.' Joyce looked serious for a moment. 'It's a big challenge, but . . . it's perfect. You needed something like this, Kirsty. You're not one for sitting doing nothing. You have more ambition than me. More energy, as well.'

'I'll need it. Carol's wonderful, though. I don't know where I'd be without her. She understands how this place works.'

'She seems a very sensible person. I like her.'

Kirsty nodded.

'What's wrong?' Joyce asked, sensing a small hesitation.

'Nothing.'

'Come on, I know you.'

Kirsty shrugged.

'It's that Bob, isn't it?' Joyce said perceptively. 'Are you still thinking about him?'

Kirsty said nothing for a moment. Then she shrugged again and looked away.

'Listen, Kirsty, you have the chance to make a wonderful life for yourself here. You're well on the way already. You'll meet plenty of other people. Don't fret over Bob.'

'It's all right you saying that, Joyce,' Kirsty said plaintively.

'Kirsty, if a thing's not meant to be, it's not meant to be. Full stop.'

Kirsty nodded reluctantly. 'You're right. Of course you are. It's just that . . . Oh, come on! Let me show you round the rest of the place.'

Problems Galore

It wasn't only the administrative arrangements that needed sorting out and setting up. There was work to be done on the building, too. Lots of it. Kirsty had always known that.

Now she began to plan ahead and sort out priorities. She wouldn't be able to afford to do everything that wanted doing immediately, but she wanted to make a start as soon as she could. For that to be possible, with Henry's agreement, she started contacting local tradesmen and inviting their quotes for different jobs.

It wasn't easy. Even to get men to come and look at the inn wasn't easy. They all seemed so busy. One or two that did come, could promise nothing so far as timing was concerned. It would be months before they could start, they admitted, even if they got the work.

She had thought she would have the place re-painted first, as an easy way to start, but the painter and decorator who came about that shook his head.

'I wouldn't even look at this,' he said dolefully, staring up at the upstairs windows.

'Whyever not?' Kirsty asked, thinking he was trying to be funny.

'The frames are all rotten,' he said, gesturing towards the nearest ground-floor window. He dug a finger nail into the window sill. 'Rotten!' he repeated.

'Is it that bad?' Kirsty asked fearfully.

He nodded. 'I could use filler as I go,' he said, 'but there'd need to be a lot of it. By the time I finished, there'd be more filler than wood. You need new windows, missus. Get the brewery to put some in.'

'The inn isn't owned by a brewery. It's private.'

He didn't stay much longer. She had

the impression she'd wasted his time. It was a bigger job than he wanted.

Carol wanted to know what the painter had said.

'He said he couldn't do it. He said the frames are all rotten,' Kirsty told her.

'Well . . . ' Carol frowned. 'I suppose they are. Henry found someone to paint over them from time to time. But it was never a good job.'

'Right,' Kirsty said, making a decision. 'New windows, then.'

'You'll have to see the planners first,' Carol pointed out. 'At the National Park offices. You'll have to get their permission.'

'That won't be difficult, surely?'

'Probably not, no, but you'll have to satisfy them that you're putting in the right kind of windows.'

Kirsty hadn't thought of that. But it made sense.

'I'm learning something new every day,' she said.

'You didn't think it would be easy,

did you?' Carol said.

They looked at each other and began to laugh. It was moments like this that took away the strain.

But Carol had hit a nail on the head. Kirsty hadn't expected it to be easy, exactly, but she had expected it to be easier than it was in danger of becoming. There was such a lot needed doing.

But she started lining up the people she needed.

The man from a windows company came and wasn't at all daunted by what he saw. Joiners and stone masons all said they would come just as soon as they could, which would be goodness knew when, of course, but was still a commitment of sorts.

She found an electrician who was a different sort of man, though. He came the day after she asked him.

He took one look and said, 'When was this place last re-wired? Never?'

'Probably,' she said. 'Not since they put electricity in, anyway.'

'I can tell you now,' he said, 'you'll have to re-wire the whole place.'

'I thought so. It will be a big job, will it?'

'Not really.' He pursed his lips and stood still for a moment, head to one side, locked in concentration. 'It'll take a week, probably. You won't be closing the place while the work's being done?'

'Probably not, no. Could you manage with it open?'

'No problem. It'll just take a bit more time, that's all.'

No problem? Kirsty thought with relief. That made a welcome change.

The electrician looked quickly round the building, then he said, 'Give me a few days. I'll send you an estimate.'

That was another thing sorted, she thought with relief.

Another high priority was the heating system. Again, that wasn't difficult. Two firms of heating engineers came out and promised estimates.

'You're making progress,' Carol said.

'We are,' Kirsty said decisively. 'That

only leaves everything else to sort out!'

She had already been warned that the building needed a damp-proof course. Along with that came the need to drain the cellars and try to make them dry. She suspected that the kitchen needed upgrading, too. Then the plumbing needed some attention, not least to stop the pipes whining and shuddering whenever a tap was turned on. Making the rooms en suite would have to wait a while, but meanwhile the existing bathrooms could be re-fitted, perhaps given showers that worked properly. And there were carpets and curtains that needed replacing.

'I'll have to do it gradually,' Kirsty confided to Carol. 'It won't be possible to do everything at once.'

'Of course not. But let's face it, whatever you do will be a big step in the right direction.'

That was true. Still, though, she worried about how far she would be able to make the money go. Even to get the essentials done was going to use most of her cash.

She would manage, she told herself firmly.

Somehow she would manage.

Just as she had worked all that out, there came the big shock. The report from the second survey, the one the man from the bank had wanted to talk to her about, said investigation had revealed that the building needed a new roof. The cost was estimated to be in the neighbourhood of £20,000. The man from the bank, with regret and a sorrowful smile, said replacing the roof would be a pre-condition of the mortgage being made available. Would she please think about it and let them know if she wished to proceed?

Frantically, Kirsty scribbled on bits of paper, doing the arithmetic.

The mortgage money allowed for some repairs and maintenance, and for some improvements, but it was nowhere near enough. She had always intended ploughing in some of the money from the sale of her mother's house, but there had to be a limit. An extra twenty thousand pounds was way over that limit, and replacing the roof could not be staged or done later. It had to be done at the outset. Dare she commit so much?

Carol guessed a problem had emerged but diplomatically kept quiet. Kirsty was grateful for that. In the end, it was a problem for her alone to sort out.

Was she in danger of biting off more than she could chew? She didn't know. She wished she did. If there had been someone knowledgeable she could have talked to, it might have been easier. But there wasn't. It was all down to her.

She decided to return to Newcastle for a couple of days and take a cool, hard look from a distance. Perhaps her plans were unaffordable. No use panicking, or getting in over her head. She needed to get it right. She needed to be businesslike and practical, not storm ahead on a romantic whim.

At least she could still do that. She wasn't committed yet, not legally. If the worst came to the worst, she could pull out.

It would earn her the undying hatred of Henry, and goodness knew what Carol would think, but if that was what it came to, she would have to live with it. There was no point in fooling herself and everyone else.

Second Thoughts

It didn't get any easier when Kirsty was back in her own house in Newcastle. She began to wonder if she had been wise to give up her old job.

She shivered and wandered around the house. It was so cold and empty here. So lonely. Already she felt it had been a mistake to come back. She had nothing to do here. It was a pity Mr Edgar hadn't sold it yet. And he hadn't. Early days yet, he had told her when she phoned. Of course it was. Far too soon. Still, she would have preferred it if he had sold it.

But then what would she have done? Stayed in a Bed-and-Breakfast, probably. Stayed with Joyce. Anything. She just hated being here on her own.

She did her sums again, and then did

them once more. Nothing changed. To go ahead now would require her to invest all the money she was expecting from her mother's house, and before that became available she would need to organise a bridging loan, if she could.

It could be done. It was possible. Matthew would help her. But did she want to do it? She was no longer sure.

She rang Joyce.

'Meet you for lunch?' Joyce said. 'Today? Now? At such short notice? Kirsty! Of course I will.'

Kirsty put the phone down and smiled with relief.

She felt better already.

'What's wrong?' Joyce asked as she sat down. 'Why are you here? Why are you not there? What's . . . ' She stopped. 'How are you?'

Kirsty smiled. 'Ready for lunch.'

Joyce stared at her a moment longer, and then nodded. 'Me, too.'

They were in an Italian restaurant in the city centre. Cheap and cheerful.

Busy. Vibrant, even. Music coming out of the walls. Waiters singing while they worked.

'I've always liked it here,' Joyce murmured, wincing as a pile of crockery hit the floor somewhere. 'It's so peaceful.'

Kirsty laughed. 'It's certainly different to Fells Inn.'

'Ladies?' A handsome young waiter arrived at their table. He might have been from Naples, Kirsty thought, but more likely he was from Jarrow or Jesmond, Low Fell or South Shields.

'The special's good,' he advised.

'That's a terrible accent,' Joyce told him. 'What part of Italy are you from?'

He grinned. 'My granddad came from Verona. Me? I'm from Blaydon. You want the special?'

'No way!' Joyce said. 'Do you do beans on toast?'

The waiter raised his eyes to the ceiling. 'Please!' he said. 'Lunchtime is very busy.'

'I'm sorry,' Joyce said, relenting. 'I'll

behave myself. So, what is the special?'

He told them, and they ordered it.

Kirsty wasn't bothered what it was.

'Wasn't difficult, huh?' the waiter said with a cheeky grin.

'Go away!' Joyce told him. 'We're busy.'

'I don't know how you get away with it,' Kirsty said.

'They think it means I'm a big tipper.'

'They've got that wrong, haven't they?'

Joyce grinned. 'Now, what's going on?'

'Nothing much. Waiting, mostly.'

Kirsty described some of the difficulties she was having, especially the difficulty of finding people to do some of the work that needed doing.

'It's the same everywhere,' Joyce told her. 'That's why we have all these Polish people here. Maybe you can find some of them?'

Kirsty shook her head. 'If only it were that simple. There's the money, as well.'

She told Joyce about the shock she had just had over the roof.

'Can it be done?' Joyce asked.

'It can,' Kirsty admitted. 'I'll have the money from Mum's house soon. I can use that. It wouldn't be unreasonable.'

'But?'

Kirsty shrugged. 'Well, it's a lot of money up front. It would pretty well clean me out. There's a lot to consider.'

'You have time, Kirsty. Take it. There's no rush.' Joyce paused and considered. 'You're not having second thoughts, are you?'

'Well . . . '

'You are, aren't you?'

Kirsty nodded. 'I think I am, yes.'

'Why? What's changed? If you can find the money for the work that's needed, what's the problem?'

'Maybe it's too much for me,' Kirsty said bleakly. 'More than I can manage on my own.'

Joyce studied her shrewdly. 'There's something more going on, isn't there? It's not just the money.'

Kirsty shrugged. She wasn't sure herself. She couldn't explain the way she felt. Except . . . Except that with these unanticipated problems, the whole venture had lost its lustre. Everything seemed different. She had run out of steam.

'It's about Bob, isn't it?' Joyce breathed, her intuition working overtime. 'It's because of him.'

Kirsty shrugged again. 'Maybe,' she admitted. 'Maybe it is.'

She suddenly felt close to tears. They had come from nowhere. Joyce handed her a tissue. She took it gratefully.

'What I would do,' Joyce said carefully, 'is have it out with Bob. I would talk to him direct. I wouldn't get in any further until I had done that. It's no use buying this place if you're going to be unhappy there. Ask him what happened. Ask him why he didn't tell you what he was doing.'

Kirsty listened but didn't say anything.

'Find out,' Joyce said, 'whether he

has any feelings for you — and whether you have any for him. Do that, Kirsty. Get that sorted before you do anything else.'

Kirsty Wants To See Bob

Later, Kirsty thought over what Joyce had said. Maybe she was right. Maybe she should ask Bob what was going on. What harm could it do?

It wouldn't alter her opinion of him, and his deception, but it might restore her enthusiasm for Fells Inn. After all, as Joyce had famously said once before, you could keep a man and your business separate, couldn't you?

Perhaps you could.

* * *

She didn't have to go anywhere to talk to Bob, anyway. There was such a thing as a telephone.

But when she phoned Carol, she was told, 'No. I'm sorry, Kirsty. I don't have an address or a phone number for him. Nothing at all.'

'It's funny, though. He was here again the other day, and he was asking after you.

'Wanted to know if you'd been again, when you were coming next, if I knew where you lived . . . '

'I told him. Bob, I said, I've got work to do. You might be on holiday, but I'm not. Honestly. Some men. They think you've got nothing better to do but attend to them.

'My husband's just the same. If I'm in the house he expects me to be working for him. He has no idea. None of them do.

'What was it you wanted again, Kirsty?'

Kirsty smiled. 'I just need to get in touch with Bob. It's urgent, and I was hoping you might be able to help.'

'Hang on. I'll have a look in the office, just in case Henry's got something on file. He might have an address for him.'

Carol was away a few minutes, which

seemed to offer grounds for hope.

'No, I'm sorry, Kirsty. I can't find anything. Henry might know something, but he's not here today. Can you call back tomorrow?'

'Of course,' Kirsty said, trying to hide her disappointment. 'Thanks for looking, Carol.'

Carol's voice became distant, as if she was speaking to someone else. Kirsty wasn't even sure what she was saying. Then she came back. 'Eddy says Bob lives in Kirkby Lonsdale. You know Eddy, don't you? He works in the bar sometimes.'

'Oh, yes. I know Eddy.'

He was someone else she had thought she would keep on, if and when she took over.

'Kirkby Lonsdale, then,' Carol said.

'But Eddy doesn't have an address.'

'Thanks, Carol. That's a help. And thank Eddy for me. I may come back to you tomorrow.'

'I'll be here. Can I ask what it's about, Kirsty? If it's urgent, I might be able to track Henry down to ask Bob.

'Or is it . . . a personal matter?'

Kirsty hesitated, wondering how much she wanted Carol to know. But it just seemed so silly!

'Oh, it's not really personal, Carol. It's about the inn. I want to know what was on Bob's mind.'

'Oh, is that all?'

Carol sounded disappointed.

'What do you mean?'

'Oh, nothing. I just hoped . . . To be honest, I hoped you and Bob were maybe getting together. But that's just me. Silly me. I must be as soft as my husband says I am.'

Kirsty tried to laugh. But she didn't suppose for one moment she sounded convincing. 'The inn is an important enough reason to talk to him, isn't it?' she said.

'Of course it is. I'm sure Bob thinks so, too.'

Kirkby Lonsdale, Kirsty thought, after she'd put the phone down. So that's where he lives.

She got the road atlas out of her car and pored over it until she'd found Kirkby Lonsdale. Not that far from Fells, she mused.

Next she turned to her computer and used a website providing a people-locating service. In minutes she had a list of 'Robert Simpson' variations in and around Kirkby Lonsdale. Eight, in all.

Which one are you? she wondered, poring over the list. And what do I want to do about it?

She sat back and pondered.

If one of these was the Bob she knew, what would she say to him?

Why did you withdraw your offer for Fells Inn? Just that, probably. Leave it there. Keep it impersonal.

She really had no right to ask him why he hadn't declared his interest. No right at all to demand he explain himself. His business was his business. It was none of hers.

But if she did manage to contact him, would she really speak to him only about the inn? Probably. It was hard to know what else she could do.

But she knew she would have to say something. She couldn't just let it go.

Surely what had passed between them had been real? After all, Carol had said he'd been asking after her recently. So it couldn't all be down to her imagination. Maybe Joyce was right. Could there be some simple explanation for Bob's behaviour?

Oh, how she wished she had Joyce's self-confidence and ability to say whatever was on her mind. Joyce would just ask, and life would be so much easier. All this agonising wasn't getting Kirsty anywhere at all.

She went into town and did some half-hearted window shopping. Anything to take her mind off Bob and Fells Inn.

It wasn't a solution. She managed half an hour or so, then it all started up again. Why hadn't Bob said anything?

What was he doing, and thinking?

What did he feel about her, if anything? What did she really feel about him?

The same old questions, going round and round in her head. She gave up and caught the bus home.

The journey took no time at all. She absently smoothed condensation away from the window and saw they were nearly there already. Hurriedly, she got to her feet and made her way towards the door. Other people were waiting to get off. People she was used to seeing every day. People who lived near her and used the same bus, and whose lives were run on the same schedule as hers.

But there were also people she knew nothing about at all, even the ones she usually smiled at and sometimes said hello to. City life. So different from Fells. So very different.

The house seemed cold when she opened the front door. The heating had not come on yet. She was going to have to adjust the timer now the days were growing shorter. Now summer was over.

She slumped in a chair at the kitchen table and wondered what to do. She felt fed up, totally dispirited.

All she could think of was Fells, and the inn. How cheerful and lively it was there, despite Henry. And how beautiful the valley was. And how good she felt when she was there. And Bob. Of course, Bob. She thought how much she enjoyed seeing him, and being with him.

Oh, how she would like to see him again, and talk to him once more.

She stirred herself. She was going to have to do something about it. She really was.

She reached into her bag and found the slip of paper with the list of Bob Simpsons who lived in and around Kirkby Lonsdale.

She pored over it for a few moments and then reached for the phone.

'Not today, thank you,' the first voice said, before slamming down the phone.

The second one was no better: 'We've already got double glazing, love.'

She made a cup of coffee before trying the next number on the list. This time she got a sensible reply, but no help.

She moved on down the list, getting into the swing of it, ruling out names.

Finally, she was left with two names she hadn't been able to rule out. Was it one of them, she wondered? Impossible to tell. Especially when no-one was answering either phone.

She sat back and considered her options. There weren't many. Two, in fact. So she either had to forget it, or do something else. And it was too late to forget it. She had too much of herself invested.

Right! she thought. This is where it gets up close and personal. It was going to have to be an in-person encounter. She was going to have to take the time and just do it.

She frowned and wavered. It was a big move to make. Then a mischievous grin broke out as she imagined Bob's surprise when he opened the door. That would be something to see.

No, she thought then, sadly. Who am I trying to fool? I just want to see him again. That's all there is to it.

The Search Begins

She drove across to Carlisle and then down the M6 until she spotted the turn-off to Kirkby Lonsdale. Only twelve more miles, she thought with satisfaction. I can do that.

But what then? She still wasn't sure.

She tried to push the doubts out of her mind. She would deal with them when she needed to, she told herself sternly. The first priority was simply to get there. One step at a time.

* * *

Kirkby Lonsdale seemed a very pleasant, historic little town. Kirsty eased her car through the one-way system in the centre, taking it slowly because of the delivery vehicles lining the streets. She managed to park in a small square in the middle of the town, next to an ancient building with a roof but no walls that she guessed might be called the 'Moot Hall', like a similar building in Keswick. Then she visited the newsagent's nearby, seeking change for the parking meter and directions to the first address on her short list of remaining names.

'Lord Street? Just round the corner, love,' the cheerful man behind the counter advised. 'First left, second right, and then right again. Halfway down the street. Left-hand side.'

It turned out to be a short street of small terraced cottages. Tidy, well looked-after cottages with freshly painted doors and windows. Quiet homes in a quiet street. On the outside, at least, Number Twenty-Three was no different to the rest.

A little girl opened the door. She was maybe seven or eight years old, Kirsty thought, and a nice, bright little thing with a beautiful smile. It was impossible not to smile back at her.

'Oh, dear!' Kirsty said. 'I think I've come to the wrong house.'

'It's all right,' the girl said. 'You can come in if you want.'

She spun round and raced down a passage, shouting for someone, leaving the front door wide open.

Kirsty stood for a moment, undecided, not sure if the little girl had gone to fetch someone else to speak to her or had simply abandoned the front door now she knew it wasn't one of her friends who had rung the bell.

She heard someone approaching along the passage. She waited. An elderly woman appeared. Like the girl, she wore a bright, welcoming smile.

'Sorry to bother you,' Kirsty said, 'But I'm afraid I've got the wrong house. I tried to tell the little girl but she was away before I could get the words out.'

'Like lightning, isn't she?' the woman chuckled. 'I can't keep up with her. Who is it you're looking for, dear?'

'A Mr Robert Simpson.'

'My husband?'

'Oh, I don't think so,' Kirsty said, feeling a little embarrassed.

She waved the scrap of paper she held in her hand and said, 'I must want the other address I have here. A younger man,' she added apologetically.

'What is the other address? Russell Street?'

'Yes. That's it.'

'Well, he's not much younger than my husband. Bobby Simpson, we call him.'

Kirsty felt flat.

'He's not a relative, by the way,' the woman added.

Kirsty nodded and wondered what to do next.

'Who else is on your list?' the woman asked.

'No-one. That's it.'

'A younger man, you said? It wouldn't be our Bob, would it? My son?'

Kirsty looked up quickly. 'It might

be. Does he go walking in the Lake District a lot?'

'He does, yes. Always there, he is. I shouldn't wonder if he'll move there eventually.'

'That sounds like him.' Kirsty's heart began to beat faster and she gave the woman a grateful smile. 'But why couldn't I find an address for him?'

'Probably because he's not anywhere permanent just now.'

'Oh.'

'He had a house but he sold it. Didn't need a house any more, he said.'

Mrs Simpson grimaced and shrugged. 'Maybe he doesn't. I don't know. He's not far away, though. He's in the next street, Pennine Lane. Number Six. He has a flat there.'

Face-to-Face With Bob

Pennine Lane was much the same as Lord Street. A cul-de-sac. Quiet. Full of parked cars, but no traffic. And no-one much about.

Kirsty stood on the corner for a few minutes, taking it all in. Then she took a deep breath and began to walk slowly along, studying the front doors, trying to suppress the panic threatening to engulf her now she was so close.

She could see Number Six. On the other side of the road. Cream-coloured door. She would cross over as soon as this man on his bicycle was past.

The man swept by. She paused and then resumed walking. A young woman had just come out of Number Six. Long dark hair, smartly dressed. She looked as if she belonged.

Kirsty felt dismayed. Her insides knotted up. Something else he hadn't mentioned, she thought with disappointment.

She wondered what to do. Then hope flared briefly as she wondered if she was in the wrong street. At the end of the pavement she checked the name plate. Pennine Lane. No, she'd got it right.

The excitement she'd felt about the prospect of seeing Bob again drained away as she stood staring past the last house, down the muddy path that led to fields, and perhaps to the river beyond. How could she have been so stupid? Of course there was a woman in his life. How could there not be? What had she been thinking?

Well, at least she hadn't made a fool of herself. She hadn't arrived on his doorstep still not knowing. He need never know what she had been thinking, and hoping. She would just get on with the main business of coming here. She would talk to him about the inn, and leave it at that. He was free to get on with his life, just as she was with hers. Joyce would approve, she thought. Business and pleasure. Two separate things.

* * *

A further shock awaited her. The door to Number Six was opened by the same little girl who had opened the door to the house in Lord Street. Kirsty stared for a moment, stunned. Then, as the little girl laughed at her discomfiture, she recovered and began to chuckle. 'Haven't I seen you somewhere before?'

The girl giggled. 'I came the back way. I ran!' Then she wheeled round and once again raced off, this time distinctly calling, 'Daddy! Daddy!'

Kirsty began to turn away. Obviously it was the wrong address. The wrong Bob Simpson. No wonder she had seen a young woman coming out of here. It was her home. The child's, as well, presumably. Now what was she going to do?

But it was her Bob, the Bob she knew, who came to the door moments later.

He stared, blinked and said, 'Kirsty?'

Then he shook his head with astonishment and smiled.

'What are you doing here?'

She smiled back, uncertainly, and tried to recover. 'Sorry to descend on you like this, Bob, but, yes, it is me.'

'Come in!'

He held the door open and ushered her forward. She stepped inside with reluctance, wondering how on earth she was going to explain herself. Wondering now, in fact, what on earth she was doing here. How had she got herself into this predicament?

The little girl stood behind Bob, watching Kirsty intently.

His daughter? *Their* daughter — his and the woman's? With a cold, empty feeling inside her, Kirsty wondered what else Bob had lied about. Maybe it had all been made up. Everything he'd said.

Things were not as she had believed. And this visit was shaping up to be even more difficult than she had ever imagined.

★　★　★

'This is Polly,' Bob said, 'my daughter.'

'Your daughter,' Kirsty repeated mechanically. 'Hello, Polly,' she added, trying her best to smile. 'I'm Kirsty.'

'Hello, Kirsty,' Polly said shyly.

'Your daughter?' Kirsty said again, eyes back on Bob.

He nodded, but he didn't add anything.

'You must wonder what I'm doing here?' Kirsty said, feeling something had to be said by one of them.

Bob smiled. 'I expect you'll tell me in your own good time. But if you don't want to, you won't.'

In other words, she thought wryly, he won't insist on knowing. It was up to her.

'Put the kettle on, Polly,' Bob said,

turning to his daughter. 'We'll have a cup of tea.'

'Polly, put the kettle on!' Polly sang. 'We'll all have tea.'

It broke the log-jam. Kirsty laughed. Somehow her spirits lifted. It was a lovely moment.

'Maybe Kirsty likes hot chocolate?' Polly suggested.

'Tea would be lovely, thank you,' Kirsty assured her.

Bob led the way into the living room. 'The kitchen's very small,' he explained. 'You can't do much more than boil a kettle in there. In fact, the whole flat's small, but it's adequate. Sit down — please.'

She stayed upright and glanced around. It was strange seeing him here, in this unfamiliar place, in this tiny flat. Whenever she'd thought of him, she'd always seen him on a mountainside or in Fells Inn. And alone. It was disconcerting, seeing him here, with other people. With a daughter and a . . . a what? Wife? Girlfriend?

But here he was. And here she was. Time to get on with it.

* * *

She decided to play it straight. No recriminations or complaints. No leading questions. Whatever she had thought it might be when she set off, now it was going to have to be strictly business. She had been silly to allow herself to be deluded into thinking it might be something else. This was a man she didn't really know.

'I needed to find out what's happening about Fells Inn, Bob. That's basically why I'm here. Henry told me it was you who'd made the offer that's now been withdrawn. I wanted to check on that before I do anything else.'

'Ah, yes! Fells Inn. That's why you're here.'

'You've got some explaining to do,' she said firmly.

'You think so?' he said, raising his eyebrows at her tone.

'I do.'

She kept her voice cool. She wasn't going to give him so much as an inch on this, whatever her turmoil inside. She wanted a proper explanation, if not an actual apology.

He motioned again to a chair. 'Sit down, Kirsty, for goodness sake!'

She ignored his invitation and remained standing. 'What's going on, Bob? Why all the subterfuge and mystery?'

'I'll just get the tea.'

She let him go. She felt deceived and she wanted answers, but she wasn't going to badger him.

While she waited, she looked round the room. She wondered who had furnished it, and who had decided on the colour scheme. Bob, or the woman she had seen?

Then her eyes fastened on a framed photo of Polly and the woman. No doubt about it now, she thought.

She tried not to ask herself again how she could have been so stupid. She shook her head. She didn't care.

She didn't really know what to think, except that Bob didn't seem to be the man she'd thought he was. Her world, was a darker shade of grey right now.

Still, having come all this way, she would at least get the business end sorted out. The rest was a disappointment she could put down to experience. More experience, she thought sadly. She should be used to that by now.

'It's good to see you, Kirsty,' Bob said when he came back with the tea 'I'm just getting over the surprise, the shock. But you're a very welcome sight, believe me. How did you find me, by the way?'

'With difficulty, but I managed,' Kirsty said, refusing to be drawn. 'What about Polly?'

'She's gone to the shops with some pocket money Jean gave her.'

Jean. So that was her name.

'Bob. I meant who, exactly, is she?'

'My daughter. I told you.'

'What you told me, Bob, was . . . Oh,

it doesn't matter! That's not why I'm here.'

'How do you take your tea?' he asked gravely, like someone's mother.

'Milk, no sugar, please.'

She watched as he poured the tea, added milk, stirred, and handed her a cup and saucer. She was surprised again. Somehow she had expected a mug, a big, chipped mug.

'Polly,' he said slowly, sitting down opposite her, 'is my daughter. The centre of my life. She's what's left of my family. Not counting my parents and other relatives, who've been absolutely marvellous, but . . . ' He shrugged and broke off.

Kirsty took a moment to digest what he'd said. 'You mean . . . ?' she began slowly.

'What I told you was true. I lost my wife and two sons. Marie and David and James. My family was gone, all except for Polly. I was never a religious man, but I've thanked God often enough for that.'

'Polly kept me going in the bad times. She was the one I had to keep going for.'

Thoughts were whirling around Kirsty's head.

'How is it that Polly . . . ?'

'Survived?' Bob gave a sad little chuckle. 'It's very simple. She didn't go on the holiday. She couldn't. She had chickenpox. We left her with my mother.'

It hit her with a sort of dull clank. The sheer randomness of it. Polly didn't go with them. So she survived.

'And Jean?'

'My sister. She helps with Polly.'

Kirsty felt tears welling up and sat down. 'But why didn't you tell me about her, about Polly?'

'I don't know, really. Fear, maybe. Superstition. I don't like to tempt fate by talking about her lucky escape.' He gave a little shrug and added, 'It's a fault, maybe. But I didn't expect you to find out. At first, there was no reason why you ever would.'

Kirsty felt she understood. She had no doubt now why he had not mentioned her before. To her, it made sense that he wouldn't want to tempt fate. Polly was too precious to risk.

'I would have done the same thing,' she said softly. 'I don't blame you at all, Bob. She's a lovely little girl. How wonderful that you have her.'

A New Beginning

Bob looked relieved. After a long pause, he said, 'Thank goodness we've got that out of the way.'

Kirsty smiled. 'So now we can get down to business?'

'If you like. If that's why you're here.'

'What happened, Bob? About the inn?'

'It's very simple. I'm a self-employed builder. Sometimes I take on an old place and do it up. Then sell it on.'

'So that's what you do. I did wonder.'

'It's a living,' he said with a shrug. 'I've been doing it since I left school. Served my time as an apprentice bricklayer then went on my own. I can do pretty well anything. Old cottages, stone walls, collapsing roofs. There's always plenty wants doing. More now than ever, in fact.'

'It must be interesting.'

He chuckled. 'You might not think so on a January morning! Some days there's a lot to be said for a job in a nice, warm office, importing furniture from China or France, while you sip cups of coffee.'

She smiled at that.

'I'd forgotten I told you about my job.'

'It made me think I ought to keep quiet about mine.'

'Nonsense. But look, what about Fells Inn? Where does that come in?'

'Well, as you know, I like the place. I like it a lot. And Henry has been wanting rid of it for a long time. Also, it wants things doing to it. So it seemed like a good opportunity. I began to think: me and Polly. Fresh start. Why not? Better than just hanging on here, trying to do the same old things. And maybe there I could spend more time with her, look after her better, instead of parking her every day at my mother's.'

198

Kirsty nodded. She could see that. It made sense.

'So I sold my house. It took time, but I sold it. That gave me most of the money I needed. The rest I knew I could borrow.'

Kirsty stared at him intently. 'Why withdraw, then?' she asked quietly. 'If you really have, that is.'

Just then the front door slammed shut, startling them both.

'I've got some!' Polly called, bursting into the room waving a brown paper bag.

She delved into the bag and turned to Kirsty. 'Your favourite,' she said, handing her a chocolate bar.

'Oh, Polly!' Kirsty stared with surprise. 'How did you know I like these?'

'Dad said.'

Kirsty looked at Bob, who shrugged and said, 'I noticed.'

'Would you like to go to the park now?' Polly asked Kirsty.

Kirsty looked down at her tea cup.

'When you've finished your tea,' Polly

pressed, 'would you like to go with me? You could push me on the swings.'

In some confusion, Kirsty glanced at Bob, who was no help at all. He just stared at her.

'I'm not sure I have the time, Polly.'

For the briefest moment, the smile slipped off the little girl's face. It was soon back. 'It doesn't matter,' she said, turning away.

'Well, maybe just for a short time,' Kirsty said.

'Oh, good!' Polly flashed her a grateful smile. 'And you, Daddy?' she added.

Bob nodded.

'We don't have much choice, do we?' Kirsty said.

'None at all.'

★ ★ ★

On the way to the park, there they couldn't resume their interrupted conversation. Polly made quite sure of that by keeping tight hold of Kirsty's hand

and pointing out local landmarks as they walked by. Friends' homes, Polly's school, the sweet shop, the café that Polly liked, all passed in rapid succession.

'You certainly know your way around,' Kirsty ventured.

'I do. I know more than anyone in my class,' Polly assured her earnestly.

Kirsty wondered if the little girl's firm base here had had something to do with Bob pulling out of Fells Inn. It hardly seemed fair to think of uprooting her when she was so well settled.

Bob offered no clues as to his thinking on the matter. He walked along in silence beside her and Polly.

Kirsty herself was in a quandary. She scarcely knew now what to say or do. On the one hand, she was so pleased and relieved to have been able to dismiss her initial suspicion that Bob had not told her the truth about his family. On the other, she still didn't know what the situation was with Fells Inn. He still had some explaining to do on that score.

Even so, and above all else, it was lovely to see him again. Now she was here, and he was here, she liked him as much as she ever had. She wanted him to take her in his arms again and kiss her. Would that ever be possible?

★   ★   ★

They reached the park and Polly immediately made for the swings.

A boy Polly evidently knew climbed on to a neighbouring swing. The two of them began to swing together, shrieking with exhilaration.

'Isn't she brave?' Kirsty said.

'Fearless,' Bob agreed, giving her a grin.

They sat and watched the swings for a while. Then Bob excused himself for a couple of minutes. Immediately, Polly abandoned the swing and came to sit with Kirsty.

'Are you going to stay with us?' she asked.

'Oh, no. I'll have to go home soon.'

'Where do you live?'

Kirsty told her, but could tell it didn't mean much to her.

'You don't live in the Lake District?'

'No. I would like to, though. Maybe I will one day.'

'Me and Daddy will, as well. Will we see you there?'

Kirsty laughed. 'Perhaps. Would you like that?'

Polly nodded and looked serious. 'I liked you a lot even before I saw you.'

'How could you?' Kirsty protested, laughing again.

'Because Daddy talked about you so much. Do you like Fells, as well? As much as he does?'

'I think I do, yes.'

'That's good.' With that, she was gone, back to rejoin her friend on the swings.

Kirsty shook her head. She hoped she had said the right things. She would hate to upset or disappoint Polly.

'What was that all about?' Bob asked.

She looked up at him and smiled. 'For me?' she asked, seeing the ice-cream cone he was holding out to her.

'Girl talk?'

'Girl talk,' she agreed.

She watched him walk over to Polly and hand her an ice-cream. The cone he must have got for himself he gave to Polly's friend, Duncan. Kirsty smiled. She liked that.

But they still had business to sort out.

'You were going to tell me why you changed your mind about Fells Inn,' she said when he returned. 'If you have, that is?'

He shrugged and sighed. 'I was all set to go ahead,' he said. 'Then you came along.'

'Me? What difference did I make?'

'You liked it more. You wanted it more. It seemed even more important to you than to me. I decided I could do without it more easily than you.'

'That's crazy, Bob.'

'Besides,' he went on, 'I don't know what I would have done with it in the long run.

'If I'd kept it I would have needed a business partner to run it, someone to operate it as an inn — and do a better job than Henry.'

'You and me both,' Kirsty said. 'I could run the place, but I would need someone to upgrade the building and look after it. I couldn't do that myself.' She stopped and stared at him. 'Are you thinking what I'm thinking?' she asked hesitantly.

'The two of us, together?'

He nodded and a big smile spread across his face. 'Wouldn't that be fun?' he said.

She smiled back. 'Indeed it would! Which brings me to another question,' she said. 'Why didn't you tell me what was on your mind? When we were talking, and I told you about my hopes and dreams, why did you say nothing?'

'Ah! That's a more difficult question.'

She waited. An awful lot rested on

what he might or might not be about to say.

'I'd grown too fond of you,' he said eventually. 'And I knew nothing would come of it.'

'Why not?'

When he looked at her and said no more, she stood up and moved to sit closer to him. 'Tell me, Bob.'

He sighed. 'You wouldn't stay,' he said. 'You'd want a better man than me. Someone who wasn't burdened by the past. Someone who didn't have a daughter to think about. Because I couldn't be without her.'

Kirsty was puzzled. 'Why would you have to be?'

He shrugged again. 'She's not your daughter,' he said.

'Why would that be a problem?'

'It might.'

'It wouldn't,' she said.

'Some people don't like children.'

'I like children. So what else?'

He looked at her again and shook his head, unable to think of anything else.

'Bob, you are silly!'

He touched her face gently. Then he smiled and reached out to take hold of her. She buried her face in his chest, breathing in the scent of him. Then she looked up, closed her eyes and he kissed her.

★ ★ ★

'Do you really think . . . ?' he began, a little later.

'I do,' she said softly. 'Whatever you thought might be a problem, I'm telling you now, it isn't.'

He laughed and said, 'Kirsty! I do love you.'

'I know,' she said simply. 'I can feel it. I have for such a long time.'

'Will you marry me, Kirsty? Eventually?'

She looked at him and said, 'There's nothing I would like more.'

He drew her close again.

'I saw you,' a little voice giggled from somewhere nearby. 'Kissing!'

Then they were parted by a small body intent on snuggling between them.

'Are you going to be my new mummy?' Polly asked.

Kirsty took a deep breath. 'Yes,' she said, looking with shining eyes at Bob.

'I am.'

'Good.' Polly wriggled round. 'And are we still going to live in the Lake District, Daddy?'

'Oh, yes,' he assured her. 'You needn't worry about that.'

They looked at each other a new, and with mounting joy Kirsty began to realise what the future held for the three of them, working together, being together.

Things do change, she thought. And for her, Bob and Polly, they already had.

THE END

We do hope that you have enjoyed reading this large print book.

Did you know that all of our titles are available for purchase?

We publish a wide range of high quality large print books including:
Romances, Mysteries, Classics
General Fiction
Non Fiction and Westerns

Special interest titles available in large print are:
The Little Oxford Dictionary
Music Book, Song Book
Hymn Book, Service Book

Also available from us courtesy of Oxford University Press:
Young Readers' Dictionary
(large print edition)
Young Readers' Thesaurus
(large print edition)

For further information or a free brochure, please contact us at:
Ulverscroft Large Print Books Ltd.,
The Green, Bradgate Road, Anstey,
Leicester, LE7 7FU, England.
Tel: (00 44) **0116 236 4325**
Fax: (00 44) **0116 234 0205**

Other titles in the
Linford Romance Library:

DANGEROUS FLIRTATION

Liz Fielding

Rosalind thought she had her life all mapped out — a job she loved, a thoughtful, reliable fiancé . . . what more could she want? How was she to know that a handsome stranger with laughing blue eyes and a roguish grin would burst into her life, kiss her to distraction and turn her world upside down? But there was more to Jack Drayton than met the eye. He offered romance, excitement, and passion — and challenged Rosalind to accept. Dared she?